MEET THE GIRL TALK CHARACTERS

Sabrina Wells is petite, with curly auburn hair, sparkling hazel eyes, and a bubbly personality. Sabrina loves magazines, shopping, sleepovers, and most of all, she loves talking to her best friends.

Katie Campbell is a straight-A student and super athlete. With her blond hair, blue eyes, and matching clothes, she's everyone's idea of little miss perfect. But Katie has a few surprises for everyone, including herself!

Randy Zak has just moved to Acorn Falls from New York City, and is she ever cool! With her "radical" spiked haircut and her hip New York clothes, Randy teaches everyone just how much fun it is to be different.

Allison Cloud is a Native American Indian. Allison's super smart and really beautiful. But she has one major problem: She's thirteen years old, five foot seven, and still growing!

Here's what they're talking about in
Girl Talk

SABRINA: Katie, what are we going to do about the homecoming dance?

KATIE: I don't know, but we'd better come up with some decorating ideas soon! We are the decorating committee, you know.

SABRINA: Please don't remind me. Hey! Why don't we meet at Fitzie's tomorrow after school to talk about it? We'll ask Allison and Randy, too.

KATIE: Okay, but I bet that's not the real reason you want to go to Fitzie's.

SABRINA: What do you mean?

KATIE: I think you want to talk about Operation Alec!

WELCOME TO JUNIOR HIGH!

By L. E. Blair

GIRL TALK® series created by Western Publishing Company, Inc.

Produced by Angel Entertainment, Inc.

Western Publishing Company, Inc., Racine, Wisconsin 53404

Written by E. J. Valentine

Chapter One

All summer I'd waited for the first day of junior high. But when it finally arrived, I felt kind of let down. Of course, everything's like that for me. I get crazy and excited about something, and, then, when it happens, it's not such a big deal after all. Maybe that's what happens when you're the youngest, with four older brothers who get to do everything first. By the time I do something, like starting a new grade in school, it's not really new anymore. The only one who hasn't beaten me to *everything* is Sam. He's my twin brother and a total pain. He *is* four minutes older, but that doesn't really count.

Anyway, I got to school late. I'm always late. It's not like I plan on being late or anything like that, but it always seems to work out that way. I got up an extra half hour early this morning, because I knew I had to look just right for my first day of junior high. But, then my brother Mark hogged the bathroom for almost twenty-five minutes. He told me he was shaving. Shaving? Please. He's only thirteen, and he probably has to shave like once every other month, but he insists on doing it every other day. It's kind of ridiculous, if you ask me. And we only have one bathroom. I mean, besides my parents' bathroom, but we're not allowed to use that.

Anyway, by then I was late for school. I flew up the steps of Bradley Junior High and ran inside. There was no one by the office. *I must really be late*, I thought. I pushed on the door marked "Registration Office." It was stuck. Don't tell me it was locked! I had to get my schedule. I couldn't be that late. Putting my shoulder to the door, I shoved it really hard. The door flew open and I went flying into the office. At least I didn't fall down. But it was not the most graceful of entrances. And I am very concerned about my entrances. You see, all great actresses are. And that's my biggest dream — to be a great actress.

No one was in the office except a woman who peered over the top of her glasses at me.

She must be the one my brothers had told me about—the Human Pencil. No one calls her by her real name, but she's really tall and skinny and her skin is kind of yellow. Her hair is pulled up tightly on top of her head in a bun and it looks like an eraser.

I took a deep breath and tried to calm down. "My name is Sabrina Wells," I said, breaking the silence. "And due to something beyond my control, I am late."

The Human Pencil didn't say anything. She just arched one eyebrow. Actually, it wasn't even a real eyebrow. It was a line penciled in with makeup. Gross. I made a note never to pluck my eyebrows.

"I assure you it will never happen again," I continued, as she thumbed through the few schedules left on the counter.

The Pencil still didn't say anything. She couldn't really be mad at me, though. There had to be other people who were late, too. I *was* trying to be punctual. It was the first thing on my self-improvement list. This summer I had decided to start this big self-improvement project. I bought a pink notebook that is smaller than my regular spiral notebooks for school. I had started a list inside it of things I wanted to improve about myself. And being on time is at the top of the list.

The Pencil finally handed me a package with my schedule, locker number, and combination. I looked at my schedule. Seventh grade seemed so much more complicated than sixth. Back then we had one teacher and stayed in one room. Now I had to change classes every forty-five minutes. It seemed really confusing. First period I had math in room 303. Yuck! I hated math.

I ran up to the second floor, where the seventh-grade lockers were located. The hallway was still packed with kids. Good, I had just enough time to dump my stuff in my locker. It was number 1701. Finally, I spotted the locker by a water fountain. I rushed over to it as the hallway began to clear out. I looked at my combination. Was it right, left, right, or was it left, right, left? I couldn't remember which direction my father had told me to turn the lock first. I decided to just grab the lock and yank. I almost fell down. The lock had been left on fourteen. Thank goodness my locker partner had forgotten to spin the dial.

I wondered who my locker partner was. I hoped it would be somebody I knew. Whoever it was had already put their stuff in the locker—very neatly, as a matter of fact. Neatness is not my strongest point. I hoped my partner wouldn't care too much about it. Even though becoming more organized *is* number eight on my self-improvement list.

I walked up the stairs to room 303. Luckily, the low-numbered classrooms were right next to the stairwell, so I didn't have to walk up and down the hallway. I slid into a seat in the middle of the room and looked around. I couldn't believe it, but I didn't know *anyone* from my elementary school. I knew Bradley was much bigger than Acorn Elementary, but still, I should know at least one person.

The teacher walked in and wrote his name, Mr. Winters, on the blackboard. Then he wrote two words that *totally* scared me — algebraic equations.

Algebraic equations! I couldn't even do percentages. I thought we were supposed to start off with rounding numbers. That's what my oldest brother, Luke, told me he'd done in seventh-grade math. I certainly hoped that things hadn't changed that much since he was in junior high.

"Sabs," I heard someone whisper. I whirled around. I wondered who knew me, since I didn't seem to know anyone. It was my brother Mark. He's a year older than I am. What was *he* doing in my class?

"You're in the wrong class," he said to me with a grin. "This is *eighth*-grade math."

What was he talking about? I pulled out my schedule card to check. Mark was right. I was supposed to be in room 403, not 303.

"Way to go, kiddo," Mark said as he patted me on the shoulder. I hate it when he calls me kiddo. He acts like he's so much older than I am. But it's only by one measly year.

The room was completely packed now, and the teacher was taking attendance. How could I stand up in front of all those eighth graders and walk out of the room? But I had to get out of there. I stood up and tried to slip out without anyone noticing me. Suddenly, I tripped over the foot of a guy sitting at the end of the row. I dropped my books and landed right in his lap.

"What's going on in the middle row?" the teacher asked.

Every single kid in the entire room turned around. I jumped up, and I could feel the beginnings of what my dad calls my body blush. I feel like I'm going to burn up, and my whole body turns red and blotchy — even my scalp. It's not a pretty sight.

The guy whose lap I'd landed in started handing me my books. One of them was my pink self-improvement notebook. Thank goodness he hadn't looked at it. His hand brushed against mine as he gave it to me and I looked at him for the first time. My mouth dropped open. He was gorgeous! He had huge green eyes and dark brown hair, just like Tom Cruise. Tom Cruise is my totally favorite actor. I have a poster of him that hangs on the ceiling over my bed. That way, he's the last thing I see before I fall asleep, so sometimes I dream about him. It's a proven fact that you can make yourself dream about stuff if you think hard enough about it right before you fall asleep.

Everyone in the room was laughing. Except the gorgeous guy. But he did smile, and then he looked at me as I started to blush again.

"Hi," he said. "I'm Alec." His voice made my stomach do a major flip-flop. I wanted to tell him my name, too, but then the second bell rang. I dashed out of the room and ran up the stairs to 403. I sat down in the first empty seat I saw—last seat, last row. I opened my notebook and tried to look busy.

All of a sudden, I looked up. You know how you can feel when everyone is looking at you? Well, everyone *was* looking at me — including the teacher.

"Say 'Here,'" the girl next to me whispered. I remembered her from fifth grade because she'd brought in these really cool Indian headdresses for our Thanksgiving play. Her name is Allison Cloud. She's a Native American. That's what American Indians are called. I remember she had explained that to us, too. That was probably the most I'd ever heard her say all at once. She's very quiet.

"Here," I finally blurted out.

"I'm glad you finally decided to join us, Sabrina," the teacher said. But she didn't sound glad at all.

"As I explained to the class before your... arrival..."

She paused before and after she said the word *arrival*. I guess she wanted to make me feel even more embarrassed than I already felt. And it worked. I felt the body blush coming on again. It doesn't really take that much to make me blush.

"...my name is Miss Munson. This year I plan to teach you the fundamentals of mathematics that you will carry throughout your academic careers."

I started to tune out at this point. Math was not going to be part of my future. Great actresses didn't need to know math. They have somebody who takes care of all their money. There was no way I could believe someone like Cher knew how to round off numbers.

"Sabrina," Miss Munson continued in her icy voice. "Are you still with us?"

"Yes," I mumbled.

Everybody looked at me again.

"Well?" Miss Munson asked. I thought her voice was icy before. It sounded positively frozen now.

I looked at her blankly.

"I asked you to round off the number 2.479 to the nearest whole number."

I thought to myself, 2.479 — *Four is less than five, so it must be two. It's got to be two. Wait a minute. I bet it's a trick question.*

"Sabrina, is it two or three?" Miss Munson demanded.

I panicked. All eyes were on me again. I wasn't so sure it was two anymore.

"Two," I heard Allison whisper softly.

"Two," I said loudly.

"That's right," Miss Munson said. She sounded surprised. "And how did you arrive at that answer, Sabrina?"

"I just knew?" I said without thinking.

"There is a logical method to arriving at that answer, and that's what we'll be learning this year," Miss Munson explained.

I looked over at Allison to thank her, but she had her head buried in her math book. Allison is very exotic-looking. She has this totally straight black hair that she wears in a long braid to her waist. It's the kind of hair that never, ever frizzes. I have this curly auburn hair that frizzes at the least sign of rain.

After what felt like forever, the bell rang. I could tell that math with Miss Munson was going to be total torture.

"Thanks, Allison," I said as we stood up to leave.

She turned around and smiled. I had to look up at her. Wow, was she tall! She could be a model she's so tall and pretty. Lots of actresses and models are really tall — or at least taller than I am. I'm four feet ten and three-quarter inches, but I'm still growing. And besides, both my parents are tall.

"What do you have next?" I asked Allison.

"Social studies," she said softly.

I looked at my schedule card. "Oh, I have band practice," I said. "I'd better hurry because I have to go to my locker to get my clarinet."

I don't really love the clarinet, but at least I'll get to march in the homecoming parade this year. It's not exactly the way I wanted to march in the parade. I would much rather have been a flag girl. They get to wear those really cute short kilts. But my family was on their annual fishing trip when they had flag girl tryouts in August. No matter what I said, my father wouldn't cancel the trip or let me stay behind. So I didn't get to be a flag girl. Let's face it, everyone watches the flag girls — not the clarinet players in the marching band. I bet lots of great actresses started out as flag girls.

Allison and I walked out into the hall.

Allison paused in the middle of the corridor.

"I have to go this way," she said softly.

"Okay, I'll see you later," I called out over my shoulder as I ran off toward my locker.

Chapter Two

I skidded around the corner and almost bumped smack into Katie Campbell. She was just about to close her locker door. Our locker door! Katie was my locker partner! Great! Katie and I have known each other since first grade. I like her a lot, but we'd never had the chance to become good friends. Katie and her best friend, Erica Dunn, didn't really hang out with the same kids I did. But I heard that Erica had moved to California over the summer. I bet Katie missed her a lot.

"Hi, Katie," I said. "I'm your locker partner."

I understood now why the locker was so neat. Katie was a really organized person. Her clothes always matched. Like today, she was wearing a pale pink pleated skirt with a pink polo shirt. She had a navy and white headband in her hair, white tennis shoes, and navy and white socks, which looked like they had been

13

ironed. I couldn't believe it!

Katie smiled at me. She is really cute. She has this great shoulder-length, honey-blond hair, super-straight, of course, and light blue eyes. "I'm glad we're locker partners," she said to me. "I was afraid it might be —"

She stopped and looked over my shoulder. I turned around. I immediately saw who she was looking at. It was Stacy Hansen.

Stacy's father is the principal of Bradley Junior High. That's why Stacy thinks she's so great. That's what I call her — Stacy the Great.

Stacy also thinks that she's beautiful. She has all this long blond hair that she's always flipping around and all her clothes are totally perfect and coordinated and stuff. For instance, she was wearing a little black flared skirt with a cropped black jacket. She started wearing a bra this summer, and you can tell she wants everyone to know about it. I also heard that she's head of the seventh-grade flag squad.

Really, she's not so great, but she is pretty popular with the guys. You'd think they could see right through her because she's such a phony, but guys are so thick sometimes. Believe me, with four brothers, I know.

"Well, I'm glad you're my partner, too," I told Katie, trying to stop her from thinking about Stacy. "I'm sorry about the mess," I apologized as I pointed at the bottom of the locker. My stuff was kind of all over. But I was definitely going to work on it.

"Hey!" I exclaimed. "You have the September issue of *Young Chic*. How'd you get it before me? I didn't know it was out yet."

"My sister has a subscription to it," Katie said.

"Have you read the horoscopes yet? *Young Chic* has the best," I said eagerly.

"No," Katie replied. "I don't really believe in that stuff."

"May I please see the magazine?" I asked. I was also trying to become more polite.

"Sure," Katie said and handed it to me.

"Oh, wow!" I exclaimed, looking at the cover. There was a big story on teens in Los Angeles. I had to get to California. If you're going to be a great actress, you have to live in California. In Los Angeles. "L.A.," I said with a sigh.

"That's where Erica's father was transferred," Katie said. "Well, I *think* it was L.A. Is

Beverly Hills in L.A.?"

"No," I said. "Beverly Hills isn't part of L.A. It's a separate city. All the movie people live in Beverly Hills."

"Well, I'm supposed to visit Erica over winter vacation," Katie informed me.

"That should be great!" I exclaimed. "You'll have to tell me all about it." I turned back to the magazine and flipped to the horoscopes. "What sign are you, Katie?" I asked.

"Virgo," she said.

"Virgo," I repeated. My aunt is a Virgo. They're very practical and they're ruled by their minds, not their hearts. That is Katie, all right. She always gets straight A's. "Okay, here's yours: *'You Mercury girls will make order out of chaos this month. But be patient. There are good things in store for you, if you can stop organizing and let your feelings lead you by the nose. Anything can happen, if you let it.'*

"Hmm," I said. "That's pretty mysterious. I wonder what's going to happen if you let it."

"See," said Katie. "That's why I don't really believe in horoscopes. They are so vague."

"They are not vague. They're only supposed to give you a hint of what's in your future," I explained patiently.

Katie just looked at me and shrugged.

"Anyway, here's mine. I'm Pisces. It's a very emotional sign and the symbol is two fish, one going one way and one going the other way." I cleared my throat and read: "*Don't let an embarrassing moment at the beginning of the month stop you from going after the man of your dreams. Be aggressive if he's a Cancer. It's your time to shine. But be careful of certain people who may try to block your path.*'

"An embarrassing moment?" I mumbled. "The man of my dreams?" Oh, boy.

"They just don't make any sense," Katie said. "You don't know any men—only boys."

"I do, too," I quickly replied. Not that I would ever admit it to Katie, but she was right. I only knew boys. And I guess "boy of your dreams" is pretty stupid. I mean, there's Tom Cruise. I wonder if he is a Cancer. It might be kind of hard to be aggressive about Tom Cruise, though. It wasn't like I could just call him up or anything.

"So what —" Katie began. But I cut her off.

"There he is," I breathed.

"There who is?" Katie asked.

"The man of my dreams," I whispered. "Don't look! Don't look! He's walking down the hall right toward us."

There he was. Alec, the guy whose lap I had fallen into in eighth-grade math. The incredible guy who looked like Tom Cruise.

"Sabrina —" Katie began.

"Shhh." I stopped her. "Oh, my gosh, Katie. What am I going to do? He's looking right at me. I'm going to faint. Should I talk to him? What should I say? Katie, you've got to help me. I don't know what to do."

"Can I look yet?" Katie asked instead, totally avoiding my question.

"Katie," I whispered. "Don't talk so loud. Should I talk to him?"

"I guess so," Katie replied.

"What should I say? I only have a second. He's about to pass by us," I said quickly.

"What about 'Hi, how're you doing?'" Katie suggested practically.

Why hadn't I thought of that? It was so obvious. And he was still looking at me with those incredible green eyes. Wow, he was smiling. Our eyes met for a second.

"Over here, Alec," someone suddenly said

behind me. I whirled around. It was Stacy the Great. She was smiling her four-hundred-million-watt smile and standing there with her hand on her hip like she thought she was the greatest thing. That's when I realized that Alec hadn't been looking at me at all. He'd been looking at Stacy. He walked right past me without even glancing my way again. Life is so unfair. I'd met him first! Why does Stacy Hansen get all the cute guys?

"Sabrina," Katie said gently, "don't worry. Once he gets to know the real Stacy, he won't like her very much. Who is he, anyway? How'd you meet him?"

"His name is Alec," I muttered. I didn't want to tell her I'd already had my embarrassing moment. "But I bet he likes her. Most guys do, you know?"

"So?" Katie said. "You're the one who believes in horoscopes. If this guy's really the man of your dreams, then be aggressive."

"It's not so easy to be aggressive," I said. "Guys don't like it if you're *too* aggressive. But this Alec seems to like aggressive girls. I mean, Stacy is practically dragging him down the hall."

Just then another bell rang and kids started bumping into us in a mad scramble to get to their classes.

"Whaddya have —" Katie and I both said at once and then started laughing.

"Band," we both said together.

"Hey, Sabs," my twin brother, Sam, called out to me from the end of the hall.

"Here comes trouble," I said to Katie.

"So, Sabs, what do you have now?" he asked, walking up to Katie and me.

"We both have band," I said quickly, gesturing at Katie.

"Can I...uh...walk with you guys?" Sam asked hesitantly. "I have band now, too," he added, pointing to his trombone case.

So Sam, Katie, and I walked down to the band room on the first floor. After I found my seat, I looked around. The band teacher was up in the front sorting out sheet music. I'd heard a lot about him. His name is Mr. Metcalf, and he has a band of his own. Mr. Metcalf is great. He is the only older person I know of who actually likes the kind of music that kids like. "Welcome to band," Mr. Metcalf said after the class had quieted down. "The first thing we have to do is get ready for the homecoming parade. It's only a few weeks away.

"If there are any flag girls in this section, I'd like them to report to the front of the room for a minute," Mr. Metcalf continued. "Everybody else, start looking at the sheet music that is being passed around."

I saw Katie stand up and smooth an imaginary wrinkle out of her skirt. I should have known she was a flag girl.

Suddenly I looked at Sam. His eyes were glued to Katie Campbell. Uh-oh, maybe Sam liked Katie. I'd read about this: "Best Friends and Brothers: The Big No-No," or something like that. But what was I thinking? I could handle it. I mean, I was mature about stuff like this. It would be no problem with me if Katie and Sam liked each other. No problem at all.

Chapter Three

"Katie, I'll meet you in homeroom," I called to her after band was over. I was really glad that Katie and I had English together next period because that meant we were in the same homeroom.

I flew out of band and ran down the hall. I had to go really badly. I pushed open the door of the bathroom and collided with one of the toughest-looking girls I'd ever seen. We both jumped back. She glared at me and gave me this look as if it was all my fault.

"Sorry," I said. "I didn't know you were there."

"Well, watch where you're going," the girl said as she strutted out of the bathroom.

Whoa…what was that all about? I thought. What an outfit! She was wearing a black leather bomber jacket, a T-shirt with palm trees all over it, these ripped jeans, and her sneakers were unlaced! I knew that look. I'd seen it somewhere.

I looked in the mirror above the middle sink. I tilted my chin up and opened my eyes really wide. Good, my eyes looked blue today. They were hazel and they changed colors depending on my mood. I puckered my lips. I had on this special lip gloss called Roses in the Rain. It was very shiny and it actually smelled like roses. I sucked in my cheeks, to check my cheekbones. Actresses needed good cheekbones for the camera.

Suddenly, I realized where I'd seen that look before. It was from a fashion magazine section called "SoHo — Downtown New York." Maybe that girl was from New York. That would be neat. I'd never met anyone from New York before.

I looked down at my own dress. It was certainly nothing like downtown New York, but I liked it a lot. It was actually the first dress I'd ever picked out and bought all by myself. I'd gotten it at the mall the week before at Dare, my favorite store. It's yellow, with purple flowers and green leaves all over it, and it's in two pieces, so I can wear the top and bottom separately. I felt very sophisticated in it actually, especially since so many other girls were wearing pants.

The bell rang. I ran out of the bathroom and up the steps at top speed. "Hi," I said, sliding into the seat Katie had saved for me. "Did I miss anything?"

"Nothing yet," Katie replied. "Hey, your hair looks great! What did you do to it?"

"Whaddya mean?" I asked her as I raised my hand to smooth my hair.

"It looks so full," Katie said. "I wish my hair would do that. You're lucky to have such great curly red hair."

"Curly hair is the worst. It's a real nightmare to manage," I said emphatically. "People always say stuff about how much they like my hair, but, believe me, it has a life of its own."

"I'm Ms. Staats," the teacher began right after the second bell rang. "I'll be your homeroom teacher as well as your English teacher this year.

"When I call your name," Ms. Staats continued, "I want you to get into alphabetical order and tell the class something you did this summer."

Oh, no, I thought. *What am I going to say?* It had to be just right.

"Winslow Barton," Ms. Staats said.

"Present," Winslow replied. He didn't have to move because he was already sitting in the first seat.

"I designed my first video game on my computer this summer. It's called Zap," Winslow said. "It's a great game. Maybe all of you will want to play sometime."

Winslow is so strange. I know he is a genius and has a photographic memory and all, but he is not totally normal. He always wears these high-water pants and he has the thickest glasses. He looks like a bug.

"Katherine Campbell," Ms. Staats said.

Katie got up and moved to the seat behind Winslow.

"We went to Canada to visit my aunt this summer," Katie said.

"Allison Cloud," Ms. Staats called.

Poor Al had to get up and move all the way to the front of the room. She sure didn't look too happy about it. As soon as she sat down, she said something, but nobody could hear her.

"Could you repeat that a little more loudly,

Allison?" Ms. Staats asked.

"I love to read. I read a hundred books this summer," Allison finally said.

A hundred books, I thought. Incredible. I'd only read five books, but that wasn't counting all the magazines I'd devoured.

Finally, Ms. Staats called, "Sabrina Wells."

"Here," I responded, projecting my voice just the way you were supposed to. I did the model walk I'd been practicing over the summer. I kept my back straight and my eyes focused on the opposite wall and pretended I had a book on my head as I moved to the back of the room and into my seat. It worked perfectly.

"I went to day camp," I said. "And I met a lot of nice people," I added. Day camp didn't sound so great, but I'd had a great time there.

"Rowena Zak," Ms. Staats called out.

There was no answer.

"Rowena Zak," Ms. Staats repeated a little louder.

"Does anyone know if Rowena Zak is here today?" Ms. Staats asked again, looking around the room with her eyes.

No one said anything. I didn't even know

who Rowena Zak was, much less if she was here today.

Then the door flew open and a girl barged in. It was the girl I had bumped into in the bathroom. The one with the New York look.

"Rowena Zak?" Ms. Staats asked.

"Don't call me Rowena," the girl hissed back.

"Pardon me," Ms. Staats said, a little taken aback.

"My name is Randy," the girl named Rowena announced loudly.

"All right, Randy," Ms. Staats continued. "Please take a seat at the end of the last row. "

Randy stomped over to the seat behind me.

"Why don't you tell us something about yourself, Randy?" Ms. Staats said.

"Like what?" Randy asked obnoxiously.

"Like where you're from, what you did this summer," Ms. Staats suggested.

"I'm from the city," Randy announced.

"The city?" Ms. Staats asked. "Minneapolis?"

"No," Randy barked. "New York City."

So I was right, I thought. *I knew she was from New York. And what an attitude.*

"The first thing we'll cover this semester,"

Ms. Staats said, changing the subject, "is synonyms and antonyms." Good, I liked synonyms and antonyms. They made sense.

All of a sudden, I heard the staticky hum of music next to me. I looked over at Randy. I liked her hair. It was long in the back, and really spiked on top and on the sides. Then she had these wispy bangs hanging in her face. It was a really cool haircut.

Randy gave me a "mind your own business" scowl and proceeded to put on her Walkman. My mouth dropped open. Nobody is allowed to listen to Walkmans during class. Walkmans aren't even *allowed* in school.

"Randy," I whispered.

Randy didn't respond, she just started moving to the beat of the music.

"Randy," I repeated, even louder.

"Is there a problem back there?" Ms. Staats suddenly asked, and walked over to us.

Randy kept moving to the music.

"Randy," Ms. Staats demanded. "Take off those headphones."

Randy finally looked up. She paused and then took off her headphones very slowly, glaring at Ms. Staats the whole time.

"Why?" she finally asked.

"Why?" Ms. Staats repeated. "Because you're in school, that's why."

This Randy Zak is a real character, I thought.

All of a sudden, the intercom started to hiss and crackle. Then the unmistakable voice of Mr. Hansen, Stacy's father and our principal, came over the loudspeaker.

"Welcome to Bradley. It's good to see so many new faces, and I'm sure you're all going to have a great year. Homecoming is a little more than six weeks away. It will be your first opportunity to show that famous Bradley Junior High spirit," Mr. Hansen said.

After he had finished speaking, Ms. Staats said, "Speaking of homecoming, our homeroom has been assigned to cover the homecoming dance. So I've divided you into groups. Let's start with the decorating committee," Ms. Staats said. "That's Katherine Campbell, Allison Cloud, Sabrina Wells, and Randy Zak. Sabrina, I'd like you to be in charge of the group."

In charge! I'd never been in charge of anything in my life. Well, I was an assistant counselor to the pee wee group at Day Camp, but this was different. Very different!

Chapter Four

Katie and I ran to our locker after homeroom and then walked down to the cafeteria together.

"Aren't you having pizza?" Katie asked as she put this incredible slice of chocolate cake down next to her pizza. It looked like this really great dessert my mother makes called Death by Chocolate. The cafeteria food in junior high sure looked better than the food they served in sixth grade.

"No," I said with a sigh, gazing longingly at the pizza and the cake. "Monday is my fruit-only day. I'm on this special Zuma Beach diet. Zuma Beach, by the way, is where all the body-builders in L.A. work out."

"Oh," Katie said.

We had reached the end of the line, where all the fruit was. I hesitated for a moment trying to decide which combination would taste the best. Nothing looked all that appetizing, especially compared to pizza. I love pizza, even cafeteria pizza. It was my absolute favorite food. I sneaked another peek at Katie's tray. I would kill for everything she had.

I took an apple and a banana, figuring that was always safe. And it also took a long time to chew. And, of course, I took some grapes. I love grapes.

"Where are we going to sit?" I asked Katie as we walked into the cafeteria. I looked around. There were twenty huge, long tables and practically all of them were full. I knew some of the kids from Acorn Elementary, but there were a lot of kids that I'd never seen before. It was really hard to decide where to go.

"Well, we better make up our minds soon or we're not going to have anywhere to sit," Katie commented practically.

"Hey, there's Allison," I said suddenly. "She's sitting way in the back. Let's go."

Katie and I headed straight to the back of the room. I tried to maintain my model walk, but it was kind of hard holding a tray full of wobbly fruit and trying to keep my purse balanced on my shoulder.

"So, guys," I began when Katie and I had

plopped our trays down next to Allison. "What are we going to do for the homecoming dance decorations?" I was really nervous about being in charge of the decorating committee, but I was trying to appear calm.

"Oh, my gosh," I whispered. "What should I do?"

"About what?" Katie asked.

"Look who's walking toward our table."

"Who?" Allison asked.

Katie and I looked at each other.

"It's a long story," I began, but before I could even say another word, I heard Stacy Hansen's disgusting voice booming across the cafeteria.

"A-lec, A-lec, save me a seat."

I turned around just as Alec turned around. We looked at each other and then we both looked away. How embarrassing!

"Excuse me," Stacy said as she came up to our table. "But this is *our* table."

I stood up. "Who says?" I asked her. Boy, did I feel short next to her. I didn't think she was so tall last year. And then I looked down at her shoes. She was wearing heels. Heels in seventh grade? They weren't high but they were heels just the same. Stacy always had to do everything first. My mother won't let me wear heels yet, she's so old-fashioned.

"I said this is *our* table, so you better move," Stacy hissed.

"We're not going anywhere," I said firmly. Who did Stacy think she was, anyway? She didn't own this table.

"This is where I'm sitting," Stacy said, "so why don't you take a hike?"

"And why don't you..." I began heatedly, noticing for the first time that a lot of other kids were watching us — including Alec.

Katie and Allison sat right where they were. I could see Katie's knuckles turn white as she gripped the chair. Allison just glared at Stacy. There was no way I was going to let Stacy push us around like this — especially in front of Alec.

"And why don't you..." I said again. Oh, gosh, what was I going to say? I could never think of a good comeback line. "...take a long walk on a short pier!" I finally blurted out.

"Whoa!" Stacy said. "That's original. Where'd you get that line from — the first grade?"

"Really," echoed Eva and Laurel. Eva was Stacy's best friend. Sam and his friend Nick named her Jaws because she's got a mouthful of braces. Personally, I think she looks like a rat. She's got brown hair and the beadiest brown eyes. Laurel is another story. She's really pretty, with light brown hair and blue eyes and she's tall and thin.

B.Z., the fourth member of Stacy's group, didn't say a word. She actually looked kind of upset about the whole thing.

"Come on, guys, let's move," I said. "I've suddenly lost my appetite."

Katie and Al stood up, their trays in their hands. I turned to leave. And there was Randy, Miss New York. She was coming toward us. The last thing I needed just then was a run-in with Miss New York.

To my surprise, Randy walked right past me. Suddenly, there was a loud noise. Randy had bumped into Stacy and Stacy's food splashed all over Stacy's clothes. All the kids at the table started to smirk.

"My outfit! You've ruined my outfit!" Stacy shrieked.

Now everyone was laughing.

I couldn't believe it. I mean, there she was in this really sophisticated, brand-new suit and heels covered with disgusting school food. The mashed potatoes and gravy were really the worst part of it. I almost felt sorry for Stacy. I would have been so embarrassed.

"I'm sorry," Randy said, trying not to smile. She picked up a napkin. "Let me help —"

"Don't you touch me," Stacy yelled. "You …you…animal. My father's going to hear about this." With that, Stacy turned on her heels and stormed off.

"It was an accident," Randy said as she sat down at the table and started to eat her lunch.

I plopped my tray down next to Randy's. Katie and Al put their trays down, too.

"Thanks a lot, Randy," I said, taking a big bite of my apple.

"Hey, she was getting on my nerves, too," Randy replied. "What's with her, anyway?"

"I don't know," I admitted. "She's never liked me."

"She's jealous of you," Katie cut in.

I almost choked on my apple. "What?!" Stacy the Great was jealous of me? "You're crazy!" I exclaimed.

"No, I'm serious," Katie said. "She's jealous of you, Sabrina. You have a lot of friends and everyone knows you. Even the older high school kids know you."

"Come on, Katie," I said. "That's because I have older brothers."

"Yeah, but that doesn't mean that all their friends have to like you," Katie went on. "She hates that someone might have more friends than she does."

"Who'd want to be friends with her?" Randy suddenly asked. She slurped the last of her milk and stood up. "Later," she announced and walked away.

Katie, Allison, and I looked at each other.

"That was really weird," I said.

Randy Zak was a really hard girl to figure out.

Chapter Five

It was eighth-period science and the last class of the day. I glanced over at Winslow. He was busy doing something to the microscope. Thank goodness we only had ten minutes left. I still couldn't get over what had happened the day before at lunch.

"It's your turn to look," Winslow said.

I was really glad Winslow was my lab partner. He won the science prize every year.

"Oh, that's okay," I said quickly. "I don't really need to. Why don't you look?"

"I just did," Winslow replied and pushed his glasses back up on his nose. He really did remind me of some kind of bug, like a fly or something.

"All right," I said. I guessed that I was going to have to take a look whether I wanted to or not. I bent down very slowly and put my eye to the microscope. I turned the knob.

I screamed and jumped back.

"Sabrina, what seems to be the problem?" Miss Miller, the science teacher, said. She was this huge woman in a plaid dress. She looked like she was wearing a tablecloth.

"There's a huge bug," I yelled. "It might be dangerous."

"It's just a fly," Winslow replied calmly.

Everybody was looking at us. I really couldn't wait for this class to end. I looked up at the clock again. What is it about the last class of the day that it always seems to take the longest, especially when it's science?

And then the bell rang. *Whew,* I thought. *Saved by the bell.* Everybody rushed to clean their slides and put their microscopes away. I said good-bye to Winslow and hurried out to the hall. I wanted to meet Katie before she left. Maybe I could talk to her about Alec.

I ran down to the second floor as fast as I could, which didn't turn out to be all that fast since everybody was in the hallway. Finally, I squeezed through and headed toward my locker. Katie was already there when I arrived.

"Katie," I began, "do you want to walk home together?"

"Sure," she replied, sticking her social studies book into her knapsack.

"Hey, there's Allison!" Katie suddenly exclaimed, pointing to the right. "She's over there."

"Maybe she wants to walk home with us, too," I said, throwing my books into the locker and slamming the door.

Katie and I pushed our way through the throng of kids. I couldn't get over how many kids went to Bradley. It was tons more than went to my elementary school. I said "hi" to some people I knew and so did Katie.

"Hi, Al," I said and smiled as we caught up to her.

"Hi," she replied softly.

She looked kind of surprised to see Katie and me. Not like she didn't want to talk to us or anything — just surprised that we wanted to talk to her.

"Katie and I were wondering —" I began.

"Oh, Sabrina!" Stacy Hansen suddenly called, interrupting me mid-sentence. "We've been looking all over school for you."

"Yeah," echoed Eva and Laurel. B.Z., as usual, just kind of stood in the background. The four of them had sneaked up behind us and were standing in the middle of the hall.

Oh, great, I thought. This probably had something to do with the disaster in the lunchroom the other day. It was all I needed to have Stacy the Great on my case all year. I might never finish seventh grade at that rate.

"Sabrina," Stacy continued. "There's something I want to read to you."

Stacy was speaking really slowly. Eva, Laurel, and B.Z. were all looking at me. I shifted my knapsack up farther on my shoulder. Something was going on. I didn't know what, but I had the definite feeling that I wasn't going to like it.

Stacy cleared her throat and tossed her blond hair over her shoulder. I hate when she does that. I looked over at Katie and Allison. They both shrugged helplessly.

"'September 1989 — My Self-Improvement Program,'" Stacy read out loud. I noticed that she was wearing red nail polish. I wished I had long nails. That was number five on my self-improvement list — don't bite your nails.

Oh, my gosh! I suddenly realized Stacy had my notebook. My pink notebook! That notebook contained all of my most personal and most private thoughts. What was she doing with it? This couldn't be happening. I wanted to sink through the floor. Stacy paused, trying to get more attention. She did.

"'Number One,'" Stacy said in this sickeningly sweet voice. "'Be on time.'"

Eva and Laurel laughed. So did some other kids. I couldn't even look at Katie and Allison. I just wanted to disappear.

"'Number Two. Be calm,'" Stacy continued in the same squeaky voice. "'People who speak slowly and don't act frantic are taken more seriously than people who rush around a lot.'"

I heard people laughing. It sounded like there were hundreds of them. I just knew I was doing my body blush. My whole body felt as if it were on fire. Why was Stacy doing this to me? Then I looked up to see Alec watching the whole thing. I wanted to die. I felt like my feet were glued to the floor. And I couldn't say a word.

Stacy went on. "'Number Six. Be sensitive' — hey, what do you think you're doing?"

Randy had appeared out of thin air. She walked over to Stacy and grabbed the pink notebook right out of her hands. She threw it at me and I caught it. Then she walked calmly down the hall without even looking back.

Stacy just stood there with her mouth hanging open in surprise.

"That's rule number fourteen in the Bradley student handbook," Allison announced clearly. "Do not tamper with other people's property at the risk of expulsion." All eyes shifted from Stacy to Allison.

There's no telling with Al or Randy, I thought. *Incredible.*

"Let's go, Sabrina," Katie commanded as she pushed me down the hall after Allison.

I glumly followed the two of them, my eyes trained on my feet. I was beyond humiliation. This was worse than anything I could have imagined. And Alec had seen the entire thing.

"Don't worry, " Katie tried to console me as we walked down the front steps of the school.

I didn't say anything. I knew that if I opened my mouth, I would start to cry. Allison smiled at me, and Katie patted me on the shoulder. I had to grit my teeth to keep from crying. Seventh grade didn't seem like much fun at all.

Chapter Six

It was Friday afternoon. The first week of junior high was finally over. Katie and Allison had come home with me to have our first official decorating committee meeting. I'd invited Randy, but she said she had to meet someone after school. Talking to her had gotten a little easier. Maybe she wasn't as tough as I thought, but she sure was different.

We walked into our living room and one of our dogs, Cinnamon, came bounding over to greet us.

"Watch out for my stockings, Cin," I yelled.

Cinnamon is half German shepherd and half golden retriever with one terrible habit: She loves to jump all over people without realizing that she's about to knock them down. She made a beeline for Katie. *Oh, no*, I thought. *Katie Campbell does not look like the sort of girl who likes dogs slobbering all over her*.

Cinnamon jumped up, heading for Katie's

shoulders.

"Sit," Katie commanded, stopping Cinnamon in mid-jump.

Cinnamon sat.

I was shocked. Cinnamon never listened to anyone. Then Katie patted Cin gently on the head. "Wow, Katie," I said. "Cinnamon never listens to me when I tell her to sit. She barely even listens to Sam, and she's his dog."

Katie smiled and blushed. "I love dogs," she said. "And I've always wanted one, but my mom and my sister Emily think they're too messy."

We walked up the stairs to the second floor, and I opened a door that led to another flight of steps. I took the steps two at a time. My bedroom is in the attic. That is the one advantage of being the only girl in a family of boys. I have the entire attic floor to myself. I love my room. It has posters and pictures everywhere. The walls slope in different directions, so the room is kind of a weird shape. I like that. Nobody else in the whole world has a room quite like mine. I'm sure of that.

"Cool!" Katie exclaimed as she plopped down on my desk chair.

"I like your room, Sabrina," Allison said as she perched herself inside a huge white wicker fan chair.

"Thanks," I replied with a smile. It's funny how well my white wicker furniture has held up. I mean, I got it when I was seven and I still like it and I'm twelve and a half. That's over five years. Maybe I'd take it to college with me or even to L.A.

I kicked off my shoes and laid down on my bed. I turned over onto my back and looked right into the gorgeous green eyes of Tom Cruise. In a rush it all came back to me: Alec... Stacy...the pink notebook...the total humiliation of the scene on Wednesday.

"I wish I could go to the dance with Alec," I said, sighing.

"Well, why don't you just ask him?" Katie said matter-of-factly.

"I told you," I cried, propping myself up on one elbow, "boys don't like girls who chase after them."

"Stacy seems to be chasing after him," said Allison.

"All we need is a plan," Katie said, looking up from the magazine she was reading. I had magazines all over my room in different piles. I never threw any of them away because I never knew when I might have to refer to them again.

"How could a plan do any good? After hearing about my pink notebook, Alec probably thinks I'm totally weird or something."

"No, he doesn't," Katie said. "He's forgotten all about it."

I studied Katie. Could she be right? I wondered. Or was she just trying to cheer me up?

"Hey," Allison said, "here's a quiz for us to take."

She waved a magazine at us. It was the September issue of *Young Chic* that Katie had lent to me.

"This is the perfect thing for you, Sabrina," Allison said. "It's called, 'Is Your Romance Too Painful? Take This Quiz...Maybe He Isn't Mr. Right.'"

"Great idea," I said. "Let's do it." This would finally prove that Alec was my Mr. Right. I mean, these quizzes were scientifically designed. They were always right.

Chapter Seven

"Don't worry, Sabrina," Katie said for the millionth time. "Those quizzes are really stupid."

I didn't say anything. I paced from one side of my room to the other.

"Katie's right," Allison agreed. "I mean, I don't even *have* a boyfriend and I scored off the charts."

"Alec's obviously not the man of my dreams," I said as I continued pacing. "I can't believe this. I think I should just give up."

"You can't give up, Sabrina," Katie said. "We have plenty of time before the homecoming dance. Do you have anything to eat? I'm starved."

We ran down the stairs to the kitchen, and I sat down at the kitchen table. That's when I saw them. A tin of my mother's super-duper deluxe chocolate fudge brownies. They are my absolutely most favorite dessert. My mother never puts walnuts in them because she knows I think they're gross. Instead, she puts in a ton of chocolate chips. My mouth watered just looking at them.

"These are the greatest brownies in the world," I assured them as I reached for the tin. I passed them around, taking a few for myself. I took a big bite and chewed happily. There is nothing like chocolate when you are depressed.

"Hey, Sabrina," Katie asked, "aren't you still on your fruit-only diet?"

"Well," I began, "on Fridays I really get to eat what I want." I paused. "It's kind of like my reward for making it through the week." They both looked doubtful at that, so I added, "I heard that if you gorge yourself on the foods you crave, you won't crave them anymore."

Allison raised her eyebrows at me. "I don't think that's true, Sabrina," she said.

"You're probably right, Al," I agreed. "But chocolate is one of my obsessions," I said dramatically as I grabbed another brownie out of the tin. "I'm what is known as a...chocoholic."

Katie shrugged. "So let's start planning," she said through a mouthful of brownie. "What are

48

we going to do?"

"I don't know," I replied. "We don't have much time."

"That's for sure," Katie agreed. "I don't know the best thing to do."

"Let's go over what we need," I said. I got up and began to pace around the kitchen.

"Sabrina," Katie said sort of impatiently, "what would we need? We know what we need."

"I don't think you two are talking about the same thing," Allison said.

"Of course we are," I said, turning to Allison. "We're talking about —"

"Alec," Katie said at the exact second that I said, "Homecoming."

We looked at each other.

Just then the phone rang. Clearing my throat, I picked it up and said, "Hello."

It was my cousin Kristin. She's my favorite cousin. I can tell her anything. She is like the older sister I don't have. She's in the ninth grade and really popular. She's also a pom-pom girl on the JV squad at her school.

She asked me how my first week of school was. "Really crazy," I said as I pulled the phone around the corner and sat down on the bottom step of the staircase. That's where I always go to talk when I need privacy. It's hard to get privacy with four brothers and only two phones. And one of the phones is in my parents' bedroom and we aren't supposed to use it. I told Kristin all about Stacy and the pink notebook and the total humiliation of it all.

I told Kristin how I was put in charge of the decorating committee. I told her the whole Alec story, including how I was dying to go to the dance with him. She told me I had to make sure that Alec knew I liked him.

Then I heard Aunt Pat telling Kristin to get off the phone and come help her with something. We hung up before I had a chance to ask her how to let Alec know I liked him.

I guess I looked a little depressed when I came back into the kitchen, because Katie asked me what was wrong.

"Well, that was my cousin Kristin on the phone," I explained to Katie and Allison. "She told me that the only way I can get Alec to ask me to the homecoming dance is to make sure that he knows I like him. But she didn't have time to tell me how to do it. What am I going to do?"

Katie and Al looked at each other and then at me.

"I've got it!" Katie exclaimed after a few moments. "Why don't I talk to one of his friends and tell him that you like Alec?"

"But we don't know any of his friends," I said, sighing. This was not going to be easy at all.

"That's no problem," Katie said. "Remember that guy sitting next to Alec at lunch? The skinny one with the straight blond hair?"

"Yeah," I said.

"I know him from the summer. His sister is a flag girl and sometimes he would come to watch us practice," Katie explained. "His name's Todd. I could talk to him for you."

"Really?!" I exclaimed. "That would be great!"

Katie Campbell was the best. I was really glad I was getting to be friends with her this year.

"I know!" Katie said suddenly. "We'll call it Operation Alec!"

"Operation Alec?" I asked. "I like that."

Suddenly the kitchen door crashed open. My brother Sam, along with his friends Nick

Robbins and Jason McKee, came barging into the kitchen. Sam was dribbling a basketball right across the floor.

"Hi," they mumbled together.

I noticed Katie blush. Ah-ha, I thought. Maybe Katie liked Sam, too.

"Brownies!" Sam exclaimed loudly. He grabbed a brownie and stuffed the entire thing in his mouth and handed the tin to Nick and Jason. I've seen Sam eat a whole tin in an hour. It's pretty gross. I don't know how he can eat so much and not gain any weight. But then all my brothers are like that.

"These are really good," Nick mumbled through a mouthful. Even with brownie crumbs shooting out of his mouth, Nick Robbins was very cute. He has blond hair and blue eyes. He is probably the best-looking guy in the entire seventh grade. I can see why Stacy liked him last year. Then I thought about Alec. Alec's in the eighth grade. Liking Alec the way I do makes me realize I'm definitely developing a preference for older men.

"You guys want to shoot some baskets?" Jason asked. Jason has looked the same since second grade. He has curly brown hair and brown eyes, and he's kind of quiet. But he probably only seems quiet because Sam and Nick rarely give him a moment to get a word in. Sam is a lot like me, even though I'd never admit it to him. We both like to talk a lot.

Anyway, I've always liked Jason. He once gave Bobby Martin a bloody nose for picking on me back in the third grade. Jason twirled the basketball on the end of one finger.

"Yeah," Nick echoed. "We're going to play Round the World."

Sam looked at Katie out of the corner of his eye and then quickly looked away. Katie was looking at me. Al was staring at some little piece of paper she kept balling up and then unraveling as if it was the most fascinating thing in the world.

"Sure," I told the guys, "we'll play."

The only bad thing about playing with Sam and his friends is that one of them always wins and then they get all macho about the whole thing. I mean, it's only a game. The guys ran out of the kitchen, passing the ball back and forth as they went.

"We'll be right there," I yelled after them.

"We can talk about Operation Alec later,"

Katie said.

"But what about the homecoming decorations?" Al asked.

"We can talk about that later, too," I assured her. "Come on, guys, let's play," I urged.

"I'm not very good at basketball," Al protested.

"Don't worry about it," I reassured her. "Neither am I."

We all walked out of the house to the driveway, where the basketball hoop was located.

"And Michael Jordan comes in for the overhand hanging dunk," Sam was yelling when we reached the driveway. He dribbled the ball to the basket and shot a lay-up. "Two points," Sam screamed. "Jordan is incredible!"

Then Sam passed the ball to Nick.

Nick grabbed the ball and shot from twenty feet away. The ball swished right through the hoop. "Isiah scores," Nick yelled. "Three points for Isiah. And the Pistons take the lead."

Jason grabbed the ball and passed it to Sam.

"Guys," I said, "if you're not going to let us play, we're going back inside."

Sam whipped the ball at me. "Here, Sabrina, you start," he said.

I walked slowly over to the first position. I was concentrating very hard on the hoop. Ninety-nine percent of this sports stuff is mental. I'm sure of it. I aimed carefully and then lifted the ball over my head. I focused on the basket.

"Sabs," Sam yelled. "Come on. Shoot the ball already."

I lowered the ball. I had totally lost my concentration. I had to start all over again.

"Sabs," Sam yelled again. "Give us a break."

"Leave her alone," Nick cut in. "Let her take the shot."

I smiled gratefully at Nick. I lifted the ball, aimed, and shot. I missed. The ball didn't even reach the hoop. I'd have to remember to put more power behind it.

"Air ball!" Sam called and ran for the ball. He dribbled it back onto the court and handed it gently to Katie. "Your turn, Katie," he said and smiled at her.

Katie dribbled to the position. She lifted the ball above her head, aimed, and then she stopped to study the basket. I noticed that Sam didn't say a word to her.

Katie shot. The ball swished right through the net without touching the hoop.

"Nice shot, Katie," Sam complimented her, whistling in admiration.

Katie blushed.

He handed the ball back to her, and she moved to the next spot. Katie looked really distracted now. She threw a total air ball.

Sam grabbed the ball, dribbled to the position, and shot. It hit the backboard with a loud thump and bounced off. Nick and I both jumped for the rebound. We ran right into each other and landed in a heap on the ground. Luckily, we ended up on the grass, so no one was hurt. We both started laughing.

"Come on, stop fooling around," Sam yelled. "It's Jason's turn."

We both got up slowly. I looked at Nick for a second. He was definitely cute. It was too bad that now I had this thing for older men.

Chapter Eight

I couldn't believe we'd already been in school for over three weeks. Time was really flying by. Homecoming day was another three weeks away and I was totally mental about the dance and marching in the parade.

I was first clarinet and I couldn't make any mistakes. Not one. All the other clarinets were counting on me. And we weren't allowed to use sheet music, so the whole thing had to be memorized. In fact, during our last band practice we had our first rehearsal without sheet music. I didn't forget anything, but then the entire town wasn't watching either. Today we were heading out to the football field to practice marching.

But I was really worried about the decorations for the homecoming dance. We hadn't really had our first meeting about it yet. True, we'd had that one meeting at my house, but we hadn't exactly gotten anything done. We were going to be in big trouble if we didn't do something about it soon. We were going to have a meeting with Ms. Staats about the decorations tomorrow during homeroom. To top it off, I hadn't been able to get anywhere with Randy. She just didn't seem interested in us or the decorating committee.

It was my idea for all of us to meet at Fitzie's after school. Everybody hung out at Fitzie's, even the high school kids. But it was *the* place to go for junior high kids. Maybe I could get Randy to come along.

Suddenly, I saw Randy walking down the hall near the seventh-grade lockers. I'd promised Katie and Al that I would really try to get her to join us.

"Randy," I yelled. "Randy, wait up."

But Randy kept walking as if she didn't hear me. I slammed the locker door shut and took off after her.

I noticed her outfit right away. Every day her outfits had gotten more and more outrageous. Today she had on these leopard-print spandex pants with a really big oversized sweater. She was wearing black high-top sneakers and a pony-print denim jacket. She looked totally downtown New York. I wished I had the guts to pull off something like that, but I didn't know if I was the type. And my mother would probably shoot me before she'd let me out of the house dressed that way. But I thought Randy looked incredibly cool.

"Randy," I called again when I'd caught up to her at her locker. She threw her books in her locker and turned around to face me.

"What's up?" she asked abruptly.

"I love your outfit," I blurted out.

"Thanks," she said and smiled.

"I guess you must find Acorn Falls kind of quiet after New York," I began. "It must be really different in New York."

"Yeah, it is," Randy replied curtly. She looked away from me and slammed her locker shut.

"Catch you later," she said and quickly turned and darted off down the hall. I didn't go after her. I had just about had it with Miss New York. I mean, at least she could give Acorn Falls a chance. Maybe I shouldn't have asked her about New York. She seemed really upset by it. Then I realized I had forgotten to tell her about the decorating committee.

"Sabrina!" A familiar and obnoxious voice cut into my thoughts.

I turned around and saw Stacy Hansen approaching. Now what? After she totally embarrassed me about my self-improvement notebook, I didn't think I would ever be able to come back to Bradley. But as much as I hated to admit it, Katie was right. Most people had forgotten all about my pink self-improvement notebook. Everyone except the Hansen clones, that is.

Every time Eva passed me in the hall, she would say something awful like, "Sorry, Sabs, but you haven't really improved." Or last Monday, during lunch, when I picked up a cookie, Stacy called out, "Number four. No more junk food." But other than that, nobody else said anything. What did she want now, I wondered.

"I heard that now you like Nick, " Stacy hissed as she stood there with her hands on her hips. She loved to have her hands on her hips like it made her cool or something. She really was too much. I thought she was interested in Alec. She hadn't given Nick the time of day since school started. Typical Stacy! As soon as she thought someone else might talk to Nick, she acted as if he were her boyfriend again.

"I don't know what you're talking about Stacy. You must be dreaming."

"Eva walked by your house and saw you playing basketball with him. How disgusting! You'd better stay away from him." Stacy took another step toward me and pointed her finger right in my face. I hated when people pointed a finger at me. It was so very rude!

"Yeah," Eva and Laurel echoed as they moved closer.

"Lay off my friend," a gravelly voice suddenly interrupted from behind Stacy and her clones.

They all turned around at once. It was Randy.

We were friends? That was news to me. Not bad news, but definitely news.

"What did you say?" Stacy asked, stepping away from me and moving toward Randy.

What a pair! I couldn't help thinking as I looked from Stacy to Randy. Stacy had on this yellow mini-dress, yellow stockings, and yellow flats. There was Randy looking tough and so New York. *Wow!* I suddenly realized. *Stacy the*

Great had finally met her match.

"I said, buzz off, bingo brain," Randy said in this really low voice.

Stacy gasped. She opened her mouth to say something, but instead she just spun around and walked off with Eva and Laurel trailing behind her.

"Randy —" I began.

Randy strutted down the hall without even a backward glance, her skateboard under one arm and leather knapsack slung over her shoulder.

"Randy!" I called, running after her. "Thanks for helping me out." I caught up with her and paused to catch my breath. "I was thinking, maybe you'd like to join Katie and Allison and me at Fitzie's. We're meeting there to talk about the homecoming dance decorations."

Randy stopped and turned toward me very slowly. "Sorry, Sabrina, but I'm just not into decorating. Maybe some other time. But I'll tell you one thing, that girl Stacy has some major problems. What a case!" Then Randy turned and walked away.

I leaned against the locker. Whew! What just

happened? Did Randy want to be friends or didn't she? I mean, she had just stood up to Stacy for me, and friends always stand up for each other. But why wouldn't she help us with the decorations for the dance?

I couldn't wait to talk to Katie and Allison. It seemed that making friends and having friends was getting kind of complicated.

Chapter Nine

I continued down the hall and walked down the steps. I made a right on Maple Street and headed toward Fitzie's. I couldn't get Randy out of my mind, though. Sometimes it seemed like she kind of liked me and sometimes it seemed like she didn't even know who I was. People in New York must be really different.

I looked through Fitzie's window. I checked to make sure that my vest wasn't bunching up weirdly in the back, and I smoothed a wrinkle out of my pants. I liked my outfit. I was wearing black pants, a white shirt, and this really cute orange-and-purple vest that I got at Dare.

The noise was almost deafening when I walked in. I squinted at the throng of kids that seemed to be crowding every inch of space. How was I ever going to find Katie and Al in this mess?

Finally, after looking around for what felt

like hours, I spotted Katie at a booth in the back. She was talking to somebody I couldn't see and smiling a lot. She and Al must have gotten there early to have gotten a booth. They were probably wondering what had happened to me.

I elbowed my way through the crowd and finally reached the back of the room. I slid right into the booth without even looking up. I was just about to tell them about Randy and Stacy, when I closed my mouth in shock. Katie was sitting there, but she wasn't with Allison, she was with my brother Sam! And she looked like she was having the time of her life.

The two of them looked at me with these sort of guilty expressions. And then they both blushed. I didn't know what to say, so I just sat there. Why were they sitting together? Sam hung out with his friends and Katie hung out with me and Al. I looked at Sam, wishing he would leave. Sometimes having a twin is not so bad. There are times when we can practically read each other's minds. Sam knew exactly what I was thinking and got up quickly.

"Later, guys," he mumbled as he disappeared into the crowd.

"We-ell," I began slowly, looking right at

Katie.

"Sabrina — " Katie said.

"Listen," I interrupted her, "we'd better start talking about this decorating stuff." I didn't want her to tell me how much she liked Sam or anything like that. I mean, I was just starting to get to know her and be friends. Maybe Sam was going to spoil all that.

"Did you ever find Randy?" Katie asked.

"Yeah," I said quickly. "We got into this weird conversation about New York, and she walked away. Then Stacy the Great came along trying to cause trouble and there was Randy out of the blue. She really told Stacy off! But when I tried to get her to come to Fitzie's with us, she said she wasn't into decorating. She's so hard to understand. Part of me thinks she's really neat, but part of me wishes that she'd stop acting so cool and just let us be friends with her."

"Well," said Katie, pausing to sip her milkshake. "Just give her time. It must be really weird to grow up in one place and suddenly have to get used to another place. I'd have a hard time, too, I think."

"Hmm, you're probably right, Katie," I said. Then I started to relax and look around. "Hey, where's Al?" I asked Katie.

"She had to go home and baby-sit for her brother. She said to tell you she was sorry," Katie said as she took another sip of her milk-shake.

"So, I guess it's just the *two* of us," I said meaningfully.

"Well, the first thing we need is a theme, right?" Katie said and smiled. "I had this idea," she continued breathlessly. "Well, it was Sam's idea, really."

"Katie," I finally said after a long pause. "I don't think Sam should help us decorate. I mean, it is our project, after all."

Katie fiddled with the straw in her milk-shake and blushed. "You're right," Katie surprised me by saying. "The homecoming dance is our homeroom's project, and it wouldn't be right for Sam to help."

"I'm glad you agree," I said. Katie Campbell was really a pretty good friend, even though she liked my brother. The friends-and-brothers dating thing sure wasn't easy, but I was definitely doing okay with it so far, I thought.

A waitress came to our table just then. "An order of fries and a milkshake, please," I ordered from the waitress. I didn't feel like dieting today.

The waitress left and I turned to Katie. "Back to homecoming," I said, changing the subject. "What was my brother's idea for a theme, anyway?"

"Well, Sam thought it might be fun to do something like Welcome to the Jungle," Katie said and blushed again. "Isn't that great?"

Give me a break. The jungle? What were we supposed to do, decorate the gym with green crepe paper and go dressed as Tarzan and Jane?

"We could decorate the gym with green crepe paper for starters," Katie said.

Before I could say anything, Sam reappeared at our table.

"Hi, guys," Sam said and blushed.

I guess body blushes run in our family. Sam's scalp was definitely redder than his hair. I'd never seen him blush this much in my life.

"Hi," Katie answered quietly and got really interested in her milkshake. I could tell she felt uncomfortable about all of this with me there.

"Can I sit down?" Sam asked, looking at Katie and ignoring me.

"No," I said at the same time that Katie said,

"Sure."

"So how do you like the Welcome to the Jungle idea?" Sam asked as he slid into the booth next to Katie.

"I like it," Katie said, looking at me.

Sam knew I didn't like it. I could tell he was about to try and convince me.

"We can cut down some trees and bushes," Sam said, "and it would be like a real jungle. Wouldn't that be great?"

Just then my fries and milkshake arrived. The fries looked crispy and incredible. They were the skinny, crunchy ones I like. Sam squirted catsup all over my fries without even asking, and he knows I hate catsup on French fries.

"Yeah," Katie agreed. "That would be."

"Katie," I said, trying to remind her that homecoming was *our* homeroom's project, "I thought we were going to do this ourselves, remember?"

"Sam's just giving us ideas, Sabrina," Katie replied. "He's not really helping."

"Yo," said Nick Robbins as he appeared at our table. Sam started to beat his chest like Tarzan and Nick joined right in. Boys were so juvenile when they got together.

"Don't you think that jungle idea is really cool, Brina?" Nick said as he started dancing.

"Yeah, real cool," I replied. I gave them all my best glare. Suddenly, I had to get out of there.

"Look, Katie, I've got to go."

"But, Sabrina," Katie said. "This theme might really work."

"Let's just talk about it tomorrow," I replied, hoping that she'd think differently without Sam around the next day.

I grabbed my knapsack and stood up. The three of them just looked at me. I pushed my way through the crowd toward the door. I reached for the knob, but the door swung open before I could grab it. And in walked Stacy... and Alec...together.

Chapter Ten

I walked slowly down the street toward my house. I was in the worst mood. Seeing Alec and Stacy together was the last straw. How could I ask him to the dance if Stacy was always around? I just couldn't believe he really *liked* Stacy.

After dinner that night, while I was doing the dishes, the phone rang: "Sabrina? It's Katie."

"Oh, hi, Katie," I answered, but not too enthusiastically. I hoped that she wasn't calling about using that jungle theme. I really didn't like it. Then, again, maybe she was calling to talk to Sam.

"Listen, Sabrina," Katie went on. "I wanted to talk to you about this afternoon."

Great, I thought. *Here it comes. She's going to say she wants to decorate the gym with green crepe paper.*

71

"You're right," Katie continued. "After I got home from Fitzie's, I thought about it, and decided that the jungle theme wasn't such a great idea."

Suddenly, I felt much better. I didn't want to have a fight with Katie about something as silly as this theme. "Well, now we're going to have to think of a theme," I said with a sigh. "Hey," I said after a pause, "Allison always gets to school early. Let's ask her to meet us in front of school at eight-thirty tomorrow. Maybe we'll all have come up with an idea by then."

Katie breathed a sigh of relief. "That's a good idea, Sabrina," she said gratefully. "Now that that's settled, we have to talk about Operation Alec."

"What about Operation Alec?" I said with a sad sigh.

"I had this great idea," Katie continued, ignoring me. "Let's go to the high school football practice on Saturday morning."

"Why?" I asked, confused.

"Well, Alec and his group are really into football," Katie explained. "And I'm sure that they'll be there. It'll be the perfect opportunity to talk to Todd about you and Alec."

Oh, my gosh! Operation Alec was really going to happen. Saturday was only a day away. I was so excited, I hoped I could get through the next day at school. I got off the phone with Katie and went back to the dishes. I was really glad Katie had called.

By the time my alarm went off on Saturday morning I had been awake for hours. I reached over and turned it off. I looked up at my ceiling and stared into Tom Cruise's eyes for a minute and let myself think about Alec. It was finally Saturday, and Operation Alec was about to begin.

Thinking about Alec made me think of homecoming. The decorating committee's meeting in homeroom yesterday with Ms. Staats hadn't really gone that well. We all had such strange ideas about the decorations for the dance. Randy didn't have one at all, or so she said. And Al's historical approach seemed just a little boring. I was surprised everyone liked my idea — Hollywood: The Silent Era — but it seemed too complicated to do in such a short time. It was a good thing Ms. Staats suggested that we use the high school homecoming theme

— Lost in Space. I liked that idea, actually. Space was cool. I didn't know what we were going to do, exactly, but I was sure we'd come up with something.

I hopped out of bed. I had to get to the bathroom by exactly eight-thirty, before Luke hogged it. He took longer showers than I did. I dashed down the stairs. The bathroom door was open. I flew inside and locked the door.

After I got out of the shower, I brushed my hair. It was really tangled. Then I combed it and clipped it back with this really neat barrette I bought at the mall. It had all these little people on it, dressed in these really cool clothes.

I must have changed my outfit five times. By the time I was finished, my entire wardrobe was strewn around my room. I looked at myself in the mirror. I wanted to get the full effect. I had on these cool green-and-white-striped suspender pants with a white T-shirt and a green jacket. I thought I looked pretty good.

I ran the six blocks to school in record time. When I got to the steps, Katie was already there.

"Hi, Katie," I said between breaths, "sorry I'm late."

"That's okay," Katie replied.

"So, Sabrina, are you ready for Operation Alec?" she asked me with a grin as we started walking toward the football field.

"Ready?" I echoed, gulping. "Yeah, I guess so.

"Katie," I said, tugging on the sleeve of her sweatshirt. It was white and oversized with these little red-and-yellow emblems all over it, and she had on these faded jeans and white sneakers. Maybe I was overdressed. Maybe I should have worn jeans, too. "I... uh... I'm not ready," I finished lamely.

"You're ready, Sabrina," Katie replied as she continued walking. "Don't be silly. You're just nervous. And, anyway, you look really good today," Katie continued reassuringly. "I like your pants."

"Thanks," I said gratefully. Katie knew exactly what to say to make me feel better. "What are you going to say?" I asked for probably the millionth time. "You're going to talk to Todd, right?" I prompted.

"Right." Katie nodded. "And I'm going to be very natural, very casual, so Todd doesn't think I'm just trying to pick his brain about Alec. I don't want to give anything away."

"Right." I nodded. "Oh, my gosh! I can't go through with this! I think I'm going to die!"

"Sabrina," Katie said firmly. "Of course you can go through with this. Anyway, if we don't, Stacy's going to get to Alec first."

I scanned the field for a sign of Alec. The bleachers were kind of crowded. I hadn't realized that so many people would be there. But I guess it was a pretty big deal. There were girls sitting on the bleachers and lots of guys on the sidelines.

"I can't find him," I whispered to Katie. "Maybe he's not coming."

"Of course he is," Katie replied. "His whole group is into football. You know he's going to be here."

I swung my legs around and looked out over the field again. The sun was really bright so I decided to put on my sunglasses. They're very large and dark and they make me feel famous when I wear them. I don't know why, but there's something about them that just has *star* written all over them.

"Hey," Katie said excitedly, "there they are. And they're walking up here."

Alec looked fantastic in an electric-blue polo

shirt and black jeans. He was so cute. And there was Todd, along with my brother Mark and some other guy whose name I didn't know. I sighed heavily. ˙

"Katie," I whispered, "I'm going to die."

"Why?" she asked. "This is perfect. Look where they're sitting."

I looked and I had to agree she was right. They were about four rows ahead of us and over to the right. I would have a perfect view of the whole thing. And it wouldn't look too weird when Katie walked by them.

"Are you going to be all right?" Katie asked me.

"Yeah," I said. "Why don't you just go and get it over with? I can't take this any longer."

"Okay," Katie agreed. "I'll be right back."

She stood up.

"Hey, wait a minute," I whispered.

"What now?" Katie asked.

"I'm not ready," I whispered.

"You don't have to whisper, Sabrina," Katie said. "It's not like they can hear you. And it's too late now — I'm going."

"Good luck," I muttered as she bounded down the bleachers and headed right for them. I took another deep breath. I had to calm down.

I followed Katie's every movement. I didn't want to miss a thing. The sunglasses were great. Nobody could tell where I was looking.

First, I saw Katie talk to Todd, and they kind of stepped aside. Then Todd went over to talk to Alec. Then Alec looked right in my direction. I felt myself blush even though there was no way he could know that I was looking at him. Finally Katie started walking back up the bleachers.

"Mission accomplished," Katie said as she plopped down next to me. "No problem. Alec knows you like him. The ball is in his court. Now, he's got to ask you."

"Oh, my gosh," I said. "He's looking right this way. Katie, whatever you said, Alec is looking right at us. Oh, Katie, I can't believe you really told Todd I like Alec. I could die."

Katie just looked at me and smiled.

"Thanks a lot, Katie," I said. "I think this is going to be a great plan."

"I think so, too," she replied, smiling.

Chapter Eleven

"I can't wait until the dance!" Stacy Hansen exclaimed.

"I can't believe you really asked him," Eva said.

"Wow!" exclaimed B.Z.

"Yeah," agreed Laurel. "I mean, he's so gorgeous. I love his eyes."

Who could they be talking about? I wondered. I was in one of the bathroom stalls when Stacy and her clones came in. I didn't mean to eavesdrop, but I wasn't about to walk out and face them either. I just wished they would hurry up and leave the bathroom.

"We have to go shopping," Stacy said. "I need just the right outfit. I wonder what Alec's favorite color is."

I almost fell off my perch. So Stacy was going to homecoming with Alec! So much for Operation Alec. Stacy had somehow beat me to it. I felt really foolish. How could I have thought Alec would be interested in me? Well, I'll just call Katie tonight and tell her I'm not going to the dumb dance! Life was so unfair. The man of my dreams was going to the homecoming dance with Stacy Hansen.

"We better go," Eva said. "Or we'll be late for flag practice."

I waited until I heard the bathroom door slam before I ventured out of my stall. That's right, I remembered, I had to go down to the art room, alone, to requisition decorating supplies for the dance. I didn't even know what to pick, since we never really decided.

Everyone was busy: Katie had flag practice, Al had to baby-sit, and I still couldn't get Randy interested. So that left me not only in charge of, but the sole member of the homecoming dance decorating committee.

I walked slowly down to the art room. I planned to get supplies and work on the decorations at home. I picked up poster board, colored cardboard, glue, tape, crepe paper, and balloons. And I had no idea what I was going to do with any of it. How I could create anything to do with outer space with all of this junk was beyond me.

I walked up the stairs and headed for my locker. I had to go really slowly because I was carrying all this stuff. I was looking at the ground the whole time in case I ran into anyone I knew. I mean, the last thing in the world I felt like doing was chatting. This whole homecoming thing was just too painful. And thinking about Alec made me feel like crying again. I just couldn't do it. There was no way I could go to the dance.

Suddenly, I bumped right into somebody and dropped everything I was carrying. I looked up. It was Randy. *Oh, great*, I thought. *Miss New York*. I wasn't sure I was up to dealing with her. I mean, you never knew what kind of mood she was in.

"Hey," Randy said. "Why don't you watch where you're going?"

I didn't say anything. Randy was just more than I could take then.

"And don't start on me about decorating for that homecoming dance," Randy continued as she turned to walk away.

At the mention of those two little words, *homecoming* and *dance*, the tears that I'd been fighting back started to burn behind my eyelids. I started blinking really fast, but it wasn't doing any good. I bit my lip to hold them back. But then my lip started to tremble. Before I could stop myself, I was crying.

I couldn't let Randy see me cry. Instead, I looked down and stared at the floor. I felt a tear roll down my cheek and watched it land on my sneaker. They were my favorite pair. They were white and had stuff written all over them from back in sixth grade. I got a lot of people to sign them one day. You couldn't read them anymore or anything, but they made me feel secure. Maybe because things were so much easier in sixth grade.

"Sabrina," Randy said in a worried voice as she put her hand on my shoulder. "Sabrina, are you okay?"

That sure didn't sound like Randy. I mean, her voice was so...so...different. I had to look up to make sure it was really her. It was.

"Let me help you," Randy said as she put down the skateboard she was carrying and started to pick up some of the stuff I had dropped. "What's all of this for, anyway?" Randy asked.

"The dance," I replied quietly as I dropped the poster board I'd just picked up.

"What are you going to do with all of it, Sabrina?" Randy asked as she bent down and picked up the poster board I'd just dropped.

"They're decorations," I said and sniffled.

"Decorations?" Randy repeated. "I thought the theme was space. You're going to create a space effect with crepe paper and balloons?"

"I was going to use tinfoil, too," I explained and sniffled again.

"Tinfoil?!" Randy repeated and smiled.

"I don't think it's funny," I said.

"I wasn't laughing at you," Randy said. "It's just a little hard to imagine space effects with tinfoil and balloons and stuff like that."

"Hey, Randy," a guy's voice suddenly said.

We both turned around. It was this really cool-looking guy. I wondered what his name was. I wiped my eyes with the back of my hand so he wouldn't know that I had been crying. He was really cute. He had wild brown hair and his eyes were so dark, they looked black. He reminded me of Johnny Depp. And I love Johnny Depp. Next to Tom Cruise, Johnny Depp is my favorite actor in the entire world.

"What's up?" he asked Randy. And then he looked at me. Our eyes locked for a second and then he turned back to Randy. *Wow*, I thought.

"We're talking about the decorations for the dance," Randy said.

We?! Since when was Randy going to help?

"What kind of decorations?" he asked. He looked right at me and smiled. I noticed he had this incredible dimple on his chin. He was so cute. I felt myself blushing. I must have looked like a total wreck. My eyes felt puffy and my Roses in the Rain lip gloss had probably rubbed off. But he didn't seem to care.

"Spike," said Randy, "this is Sabrina. Sabrina, Spike."

Spike, I thought. *What an incredibly cool name.* He looked like he could be a rock star. *Wow.*

"So, Sabrina," Spike said. "Are you going to the dance?"

"Yeah, I guess so," I blurted out, forgetting that just a few minutes ago I was miserable and had hated the idea of having to go to the dance. Now, it didn't seem like such a bad idea.

"Good," he said. "Then you'll hear my band play."

That's right, I thought. Spike *was* a rock star.

His band was doing our dance.

"Spike plays lead guitar and sings for Wide Awake, the ninth-grade band," Randy explained.

"What's all this stuff for?" Spike asked, gesturing at all the things I'd picked out in the art room.

"Uh...I don't know," I admitted. "It's...uh ...kind of dance decorating stuff."

That was a sparkling answer. I was really being a witty conversationalist or whatever those magazines were always saying. Spike probably thought I was totally dizzy.

"Hey, I've got to run," Spike said. "Catch you later, Randy. See you at the dance, Sabrina."

He looked at me once more and then he was gone.

"Wow!" I breathed to Randy. "He's incredible."

"I know," she agreed. "So's his music. It reminds me of my favorite band back in New York, Broken Arrow."

"Are you going out with him?" I asked Randy.

"Me and Spike?" Randy asked incredulously. She started to laugh. "I don't believe in all that couples stuff. Do you?"

I shook my head and said no, even though I

wasn't exactly sure whether I did or not.

"So, back to the decorating," Randy said. "The homecoming theme is space, right?"

"Yeah," I agreed. "Lost in Space."

"So, do you have any ideas besides the tinfoil?" Randy asked.

"Well, no, not really," I answered.

"I have a great idea!" Randy suddenly exclaimed. "I have these really cool lights. I could hook them up to my light organ and get them to flash to the beat of the music."

This is different, I thought. I mean, I didn't know what a light organ was, but it sure sounded better than crepe paper and balloons. "And," Randy continued, "I'm sure Spike would let us use one of Wide Awake's smoke machines if we ask him."

"Great!" I said. I couldn't really figure out what Randy was planning to do with all the lights and how it was going to look. But she sure seemed psyched to do it. I guess it was worth a shot.

"The gym will look sort of like a spaceship with mist and weird lights," Randy explained. "That's the idea. Anyway, I've got to go. Talk to you tomorrow."

"Okay," I said and grinned. "Bye, Randy! Thanks."

Randy turned and flipped her skateboard onto her shoulder and strolled down the hall.

I couldn't wait to tell Katie and Al about Randy, the lights, and the smoke machine. But one thing for sure, they were absolutely going to *die* when they heard about Spike.

Chapter Twelve

I had never been so nervous in my life. I mean, being first clarinet in the homecoming parade was a big deal. And billions of people would be out there watching me. I was trying to get in a few final moments of practice, but it was kind of hard since everybody else in the parade was trying to do the same thing. There was a lot of noise with all the instruments going at once, and it sounded so off-key.

I glanced down at my watch. It was almost five o'clock on Friday, and we were supposed to start marching at five. The day of the big homecoming parade had finally arrived. Everybody in the whole entire town of Acorn Falls was lining the streets. The football game against our biggest rivals, the Alma Redwings, was right after the parade. The Acorn Wolves just had to beat the Redwings this year.

"Hey, Sabrina," Nick Robbins called as he

walked over. He was holding this big bass drum and two huge sticks. "Ready for the parade?"

I nodded, but I couldn't say anything because I had the reed from my clarinet in my mouth. I knew I must look really stupid, except that every good clarinet player knows that you have to wet your reed for at least ten minutes before you play. That's what the professionals do. Otherwise, you squeak.

"Too bad we can't march together," Nick continued. "We'd have a great time." He smiled at me, his blue eyes lighting up. *Gosh, is he cute,* I thought, but he really was too young for me.

I nodded and tried to smile back, except as soon as I moved my lips, my reed fell out. "Ooops," I said.

Nick and I both went to grab it. He knocked into me with his huge drum, and I fell backward onto the grass.

"Sabrina, I'm sorry," Nick apologized as he helped me up. "I keep forgetting this drum is so big."

I brushed off my pants, and we both laughed. Nick handed me my reed. How embarrassing! It was all wet with my saliva. And he had touched it. Gross! I wiped it off and put it back in my mouth.

"Sabrina," Nick said nervously. "There's … uh … something I…uh…want to ask you."

He didn't say anything for a minute. I just sucked on my reed. Nick sure looked nervous. I guess this parade was really getting to him. After all, he was the only bass drum. He must be under a lot of pressure.

"I was…uh…wondering… uh…if you… uh …" Nick's voice trailed off.

I looked at him and waited. What was taking him so long? I couldn't say anything, of course, because of my reed.

"Sabrina," Nick began again, looking down. He blushed.

Gosh, did he look cute when he blushed, just like a little boy.

"Doyouwannagotothehomecomingdance withme?" Nick finally blurted out so fast that it took me a moment to figure out what he'd said.

Before I could answer, Mr. Metcalf blew his whistle and everybody started to line up.

"Catch you at the end of the parade," Nick muttered as he hurried over to the drum section.

I just stood there for a second, my reed in my hand. *Oh, my gosh*, I thought, Nick Robbins had just asked me to go to the homecoming dance with him. Now what was I going to do? Last year I probably would have killed to have Nick ask me out. Now, though, seventh-grade boys seemed so young. And I didn't exactly *like* Nick. I really only liked him as a friend. And I didn't want things to get messed up.

"Sabrina!" Mr. Metcalf yelled, interrupting my thoughts. "Over here. Everybody, positions please."

Winslow, of course, bumped into me as soon as he got into his position, which happened to be directly behind me. He was the number-seven clarinet. "Ummm, Winslow," I began, as tactfully as I could, "try to stay in step, okay?"

He just made this goofy face at me and nodded.

Suddenly the trombone section at the front of the formation began to move, but then they stopped again. All this waiting was so frustrating! I wondered how Sam was doing. He wasn't too thrilled about marching. He didn't really like having people watch him do stuff except play sports.

I caught a glimpse of black-and-orange plaid as the flag girls did their warm-up in the very front. Katie was so lucky to be a flag girl, even though she thought it was no big deal. This year their outfits were really cute. They had on these short plaid kilts, black turtlenecks, plaid sashes, and plaid berets. The berets were kind of dorky, but I thought they added a nice touch. Anyway, Katie said that Stacy was such a pain and was always pushing up toward the front. It figured. Stacy always had to be the center of attention, no matter what.

I took a deep breath, and wiped the palms of my hands on my pants. I guess I was pretty nervous. I hoped I looked okay, though. I hadn't exactly had much choice about what to wear, and our outfits definitely weren't cute. Every single band person in every squad had on black pants with white shirts. We looked like a bunch of penguins or something.

"Sabrina," Winslow whispered loudly.

It was time for my squad to start moving. I raised my clarinet and put the end piece in my mouth. And before I knew it, we were marching. It was totally different from rehearsal. All we did then was march around the football field. Now we were marching down the street with people watching.

We reached the center of town and the parade came to a halt. The drums started a cadence solo. Suddenly the varsity cheerleaders came popping out of the rocket on the senior float. They lined up in front of the bleachers along the street right where the mayor was standing. In time with the beat of the drums, the cheerleaders waved their pom-poms and did one of my favorite cheers: "We've got the coach, we've got the team, we've got the pep, we've got the steam, fifteen big ones for our team — rah rah, rah rah rah, rah rah, rah rah rah!" Then all the spectators answered their cheer with "Go Wolves, go!"

It was almost time for the big finale. I noticed that it had become really windy all of a sudden. The flag girls' skirts were blowing around and a couple of them lost their berets. They looked like they were kind of having a hard time. I mean, they weren't even twirling their flags. They were just holding on to them for dear life.

Then a huge gust of wind came just as the flag girls were about to start their big balloon routine. They should have just forgotten about it. Their balloons had already begun to float away into the sky. Then some of the flag girls actually dropped their flags. Everybody started laughing, even a lot of the flag girls — including Katie. But Stacy Hansen looked really mad, especially when her skirt blew straight up. It made me kind of glad that I was a clarinet player. The wind wasn't about to blow my instrument away.

Everybody clapped after the flag girls finished, not that they really finished anything. We marched the rest of the way down Main Street and made a right turn at the end. I could see our school just up ahead. Time was running out. Nick had said he would talk to me at the end of the parade and the parade was almost over. I had to make a decision. What was I going to do? I needed to talk to Katie first.

We marched onto the football field and then Mr. Metcalf blew his whistle. The parade was officially over. I tucked my clarinet under my arm and frantically looked around for Katie. I had to talk to her before Nick found me. But there were kids swarming all over the place. And I didn't see Katie anywhere.

"Sabrina," someone yelled. "Yo, Sabrina."

I turned around. It was Nick. Well, so much

for talking to Katie. I was just going to have to make up my *own* mind. The only thing was, I still had no idea what to do.

"How'd you do?" Nick asked me. He smiled. "It wasn't as bad as I thought. That wind was something, huh?"

"Yeah," I said. I shifted my weight from one foot to the other. I had to make up my mind in a matter of seconds. I could feel that he was about to pop the big question. Yipes!

"So, Sabrina," Nick began again.

This sounded as if it was going to be the moment. I gulped again.

"Do you wanna go to the dance with me?" Nick finally asked in this soft voice. Then he blushed. He looked so cute.

"Sure, Nick, I'd love to," I blurted out before I could think about it for another second.

Chapter Thirteen

"Sabrina," Randy commanded, "put one klieg light in each corner." It was Saturday afternoon and Randy, Katie, Allison, and I were trying to get the gym decorated in time for the dance that night. We had been there for over an hour already, and I didn't think we would ever finish.

I went over to the stack of lights Randy and Allison had brought over that morning. I stood there, confused, looking down at all the weird, high-tech-looking lights. What the heck was a klieg light, anyway? I couldn't really tell one light from another. I mean, I couldn't even tell where one light ended and another began.

"What's the problem, Sabrina?" Randy asked, looking up from this box that looked like my brother's stereo. She said it was called a light organ. It definitely didn't look like an organ to me. It didn't even have keys on it.

I looked at Randy helplessly. Then Al walked over to me and pointed at something that looked like a black paint can on a really tall stand.

"That's a klieg light, Sabrina," Al informed me.

"How'd you know that?" I asked, surprised.

She opened her mouth to answer, but I cut her off. "No, forget it, don't tell me. You got it from some book."

"They use them in movies," Al continued.

"Really?" I asked, turning to Randy. Movies. Now *this* was interesting.

"Yeah," Randy said as she looked up at me.

"Really?" I repeated. "Where'd you get these from, Randy?"

Al and Katie looked at her. Randy didn't say anything. I was about to ask her again, when she finally said, "My father."

"Your father?" I asked, puzzled. Why would her father give her these lights?

"Yeah," Randy said. "He's a director."

"A director!" Katie and I exclaimed at the same time. I couldn't believe my luck. Randy had a director for a father, and here I was wanting to be an actress. This only happened in the movies. "What movies has he done?" I asked.

"He doesn't do movies," Randy explained, turning back to her fiddling with the light organ. "He directs commercials and rock videos."

"Wow!" I exclaimed. "That's wild. Have I seen any?"

"Probably," Randy replied, distractedly. "Al, could you hand me that red wire by your feet?"

I really wanted to ask Randy more about her father, but she was obviously too busy to talk. Katie nudged me, and we both picked up one of the klieg lights. I definitely looked at it differently now. I wondered what stars had stood in front of it. I would have to find out. Carrying it over to the corner, I put my fingers on the light bulb.

"Sabrina!" Randy yelled, startling me. I almost dropped the light.

"What?" I asked, a little annoyed. Why did she have to scare me like that?

"Sorry, Sabs," Randy apologized. "But you should never touch a halogen light bulb like that. The oil on your fingers can burn it out."

"Oh," I replied.

Katie and I set up all four lights in the corners and went back to the middle of the gym. "What are we going to do with all these other lights?" Katie asked Randy.

"Well," Randy began, thinking. "You could take all those spotlights and line them up. They're colored, so put the colors that go best together next to each other."

Katie and I pulled out all the spotlights and started arranging them in front of the stage. Randy thought it would be pretty cool to set them up on the stage. I did, too. Randy really knew a lot about these lights. And so did Allison.

"Sabrina," Katie began, "I'm so glad you're going to the dance with Nick. We can double or something. Aren't you excited?"

"Double!" I cried. "Who are you going to the dance with?"

"Sam," Katie mumbled, and stared at the floor.

"Why didn't you tell me this before? I mean, we talk on the phone every day," I said to Katie. I was starting to get a little upset now.

"Well," Katie began slowly, "I thought you'd get upset. You act a little strange every time I mention Sam. Besides, this isn't a date or anything. We're going with all of you."

I just shrugged my shoulders and told Katie it was okay. I didn't know what else to say. I guess I didn't expect my brother Sam to be taking Katie to the dance. It was weird.

"Sabrina," Allison suddenly called. She was on top of a ladder. "Can you hand me one of those spots?"

I handed Allison the spots one at a time, and she clipped them to this long bar above the stage. I was glad to have something else to do. I didn't want to hear any more about Katie and Sam.

Randy walked over to us when we were finished. She had those long tube things with her. "These are called tracers," she said. "The bulbs light up in sequence so it looks like the light is actually moving. Help me tape these up around the stage."

"Wild!" I exclaimed. This *was* going to be really cool.

"You haven't seen anything," Randy said with a grin. "We haven't hooked them up yet. We just have to wait for Spike to show up with his sound board and tape machine."

Spike?! Spike was coming here? Today? And

then, talk about timing, the door slammed open and Spike sauntered in, carrying all this stereo stuff.

"Hey, guys," he called out, putting everything down on the stage. "How's it going?"

He looked right at me when he said that. Spike was so cool. Katie was just standing there staring at him. I could tell she thought Spike was really cool, too.

Spike asked me to help them hook everything up. The big black boxes that were on the corner of the stage turned out to be speakers. Then Randy started feeding the wires from her equipment to Spike, and he attached them to his stuff.

Finally, everything was in place. "You guys, come out to the middle of the floor," Randy ordered as she jumped off the stage. "We'll get a better effect out there."

Everyone — except Spike — stood in the middle of the floor, waiting. "Well?" Randy asked impatiently.

Unbelievable! It was absolutely the coolest thing I had ever seen. The music was blaring from the speakers, and the lights were blinking on and off. They were all blinking at different times, but they all seemed to go with the beat of the music. Randy had explained that the light organ filtered the sound into different frequencies and fed that to the lights, or something like that. I didn't quite understand it, but it looked totally wild. And it seemed as if the light was really moving around the stage.

"Cool music, Randy," Spike called over the beat. "Who is it?"

"My friends from New York, Broken Arrow," Randy said. "You can borrow it if you want."

"Hey!" Spike said suddenly. "What about the smoke machine? You know, you should attach the machine to the ceiling, so the smoke will come down instead of go up. It's a better effect."

"You're right, you're right," Randy agreed.

"It's definitely more dramatic," Spike added. "What do you think, Sabrina?"

"Definitely more dramatic," I replied. "Definitely."

"Definitely," Spike repeated, fixing his black eyes on me. "If Sabrina's definite, then that's the way to go.

"Listen, Randy," he said, never taking his

eyes from me, "you need to adjust those kliegs. They're all over the place."

Randy agreed and went over to one of the corners.

"Test them on Sabrina," he continued. Then he said, "Hey, Sabrina, how about we do some dancing so that Randy can test the lights?"

"Whaddya mean?" I asked.

"Well, you do know how to dance, don't ya? "Spike asked, in a teasing voice.

"Sure," I said, smiling.

Randy jumped up onto the stage. "I'll put something on I'm sure you'll like," she shouted and switched tapes. She went back to the klieg light in the front corner and started fiddling with the stand.

"She Drives Me Crazy" came blaring out of the speakers. Spike and I stood in the middle of the gym facing each other. The lights began pulsating to the beat of the music again, and the effect was totally unreal. The gym seemed like it was a million miles away. I really felt like I was lost in space.

I just loved this song, too. How did Randy know? It was one of my absolute favorites. Even though I was really nervous about dancing with Spike, I loved the music, and Spike was an incredible dancer.

Suddenly the doors flew open. Nick and Jason came in with some boxes. All at once, the song ended, the music stopped, and the lights went out.

"I thought you guys were decorating," Nick said in this obnoxious voice. "It doesn't look like you're doing any work to me." He frowned.

Nick definitely looked mad. I'd never seen him mad before. I wondered what was wrong.

"Hey, Nick, do you know Spike?" I asked.

"No, I don't know 'Spike,'" Nick practically spat out. "Who's Spike?"

"I am," Spike said. "It's good to meet..." His voice trailed off.

"Nick," he barked as he moved toward Spike. Spike just leaned back on his heels and grinned. Something was definitely going on. Something intense.

Nick started blinking really hard. He was practically glaring at Spike. Spike kept grinning.

I stood still, totally confused by what was happening.

I'd never seen Nick act like this before, and I had known him practically forever. I didn't know what to do.

"I'll call you later, Sabrina," Nick finally said, as he and Jason stalked out of the gym.

I looked at Katie, who looked at me helplessly. Allison was busy moving the ladder under the basketball backboard to hang up the smoke machine. And Randy just shrugged. How did everything always get so complicated? I wondered.

Chapter Fourteen

Nick calls Sabrina

NICK: Hi, Sabrina. It's Nick. There's
           something I've got to tell you.
SABRINA: Hi, Nick. What?
NICK: It's about the homecoming dance.
SABRINA: Well, what about it?
NICK: I don't want to go with you any-
           more.
SABRINA: WHAT???!!!
NICK: You heard me.
SABRINA: What are you talking about?
NICK: I said, I don't want to go to home-
           coming with you anymore, that's
           all.
SABRINA: Nick, what's wrong with you? I
           want to go to the dance with you.
NICK: Well, I don't want to go with you.
SABRINA: Come on, Nick. The dance is

	tonight.
NICK:	Yeah, well, I think I'm going with someone else.
SABRINA:	Someone else! You already asked me!
NICK:	Yeah, well, I've changed my mind.
SABRINA:	Oh, I see.
NICK:	Listen, I've got to go. Catch you later.
SABRINA:	Sure. Bye.

Sabrina calls Katie

SABRINA:	Katie. My life is over!
KATIE:	Sabrina? Is that you? What's wrong? The dance is only a few hours away.
SABRINA:	I know. I can't go.
KATIE:	Sabs, what are you talking about?
SABRINA:	It's too awful. You're going to die when you hear it.
KATIE:	Sabrina, just tell me!!!
SABRINA:	Nick Robbins called me. He's taking someone else to homecoming. He dumped me. And practically the entire school knows I'm going

	with him and now he's going with someone else. There's no way I can show my face in public tonight.
KATIE:	Why would he do that?
SABRINA:	I don't know. That's what I keep asking myself. I thought he liked me.
KATIE:	Oh. Well, I told you these friend things never work out.
SABRINA:	Please, Katie. I don't want to get into that right now. It's just too painful. I can't even think about it.
KATIE:	Oh, my gosh, Sabrina! Nick must be jealous. *That's* why he canceled on you. He's jealous of Spike and that whole thing this afternoon.
SABRINA:	What???!!!
KATIE:	Don't be dense, Sabrina. I mean, think about it for a minute. He walked into the gym today and found you dancing with another guy! Of course he's jealous.
SABRINA:	I don't know about that. Anyway, it doesn't matter. I've been dumped. Now I don't want to go

to this stupid dance!

KATIE: But, Sabrina, you have to go. You can't let a stupid guy stop you from having fun.

SABRINA: I just can't, Katie. It's just too embarrassing. I can't do it.

KATIE: Well, at least think about it, okay? I'll call you later.

SABRINA: I won't change my mind.

KATIE: Well, just think about it. Talk to you later. Bye.

SABRINA: Bye.

Katie calls Allison

KATIE: Hello, can I speak to Allison, please?

CHARLIE: Are you a spy?

(Static, then a loud bang, and finally, Allison picks up the phone.)

ALLISON: Hello.

KATIE: Allison? Hi. It's Katie. I have to talk to you. Do you have a minute?

ALLISON: Sure. Sorry about Charlie. You'd never know he was seven. He acts

	like a two-year-old. And he's always picking up the phone before anyone else can get to it.
KATIE:	That's okay. Listen, we have to do something about Sabrina.
ALLISON:	Why? What happened? What's wrong with her?
KATIE:	It's kind of complicated. Remember when Nick walked into the gym this afternoon and Spike and Sabrina were dancing? Well, Nick just called Sabrina and he told her he doesn't want to go to the dance with her anymore. Plus, he said he's already asked someone else.
ALLISON:	Oh, no! That's terrible. She must be really upset.
KATIE:	She is. She said she can never show her face in public ever again so she's not going to go to the dance at all.
ALLISON:	Sabrina has to go. I didn't want to go at first and she talked *me* into going. I'm sure she'll have a good time at the dance anyway.

KATIE: That's what I said. But she didn't listen to me.

ALLISON: Well, Nick was certainly mad at Spike this afternoon. That was obvious. He probably told Sabrina he wouldn't go with her because he's afraid Sabrina likes Spike more than she likes him.

KATIE: That's exactly what I told her, Al.

ALLISON: So what are we going to do? She's got to go tonight.

KATIE: Well, she won't listen to me. I don't know what to do.

ALLISON: Well, let me call Randy. Sabrina might listen to her.

KATIE: Good idea. Let me know what happens. Talk to you later. Bye.

ALLISON: Bye.

Allison calls Randy

ALLISON: Randy? This is Allison. Allison Cloud.

RANDY: Hi, Al. What's up?

ALLISON: Katie just called me and told me that Sabrina isn't going to the homecoming dance because Nick Robbins called and told her that he doesn't want to go with her anymore, and that he's taking someone else instead.

RANDY: Well! Things on the Acorn Falls dating scene really move quickly. *(Randy laughs.)*

ALLISON: Well, we have to do something. Sabrina won't listen to Katie, and I thought maybe you could talk to her. Sabrina is completely distraught.

RANDY: Well, I guess I could call her. There's no way I'm going to let her back out now.

ALLISON: Right. Thanks, Randy.

RANDY: *Ciao.*

ALLISON: Good-bye, Randy.

Randy calls Sabrina

RANDY: Hey, is Sabrina around?

SAM: Yeah. Who's this?

RANDY: Randy. Who's this?

SAM: Sam. Hi, Randy. Hold on a sec.

(Sam drops the phone and yells, "Bla-abs, phone!")

SABRINA: Hello.

RANDY: Six o'clock. My house. Be there.

SABRINA: Randy? What are you talking about?

RANDY: We've got a lot to do to get ready for the big dance tonight.

SABRINA: Randy, I have to tell you something *(pause)*. I can't go to the dance *(heavy sigh)*.

RANDY: Get a grip, Sabrina. So, I'll see you at six. My house is the one on the corner of Maple and Ninth.

SABRINA: Randy, you don't understand. I've been stood up. I can't go to this dance. The embarrassment of it all will kill me.

RANDY: Give me a break. Anyway, this way you can hang with me and Allison and Spike and the band. It'll be really cool.

SABRINA: Well, that's true.

RANDY: I'll see you at six. *Ciao.*

Chapter Fifteen

It was Saturday night. The night of the big dance. The gym looked incredible. Lights were flashing to the beat of the music. Wide Awake was a really good band. They were playing great dance music. Not that a lot of kids were dancing — except for some of the girls. Most of the guys were standing around in these little groups, hanging out. Randy had done an amazing job. All of her high-tech light stuff had really saved us. Everybody seemed to love the effects, and we hadn't even used the smoke machine yet. The decorating committee was definitely a hit.

A slow song started playing. It was the first slow song of the night. There was Katie dancing with Sam, and I hadn't even had a chance to talk to her yet. I had to admit, though, that they looked pretty cute together. She was wearing a great outfit, of course — this blue-and-white-striped mini-dress with little blue flats and a blue-and-white headband. And Sam was actually wearing a pair of jeans without holes in the knees. I think he had even put on some of our brother Luke's cologne — Wild Spice, or something like that.

All of a sudden, I saw a flash of blond hair and Nick standing in a corner talking to Eva Malone. Eva Malone! *What a couple of twerps,* I thought.

That's when I saw Alec. He had his arms around Stacy and he was smiling at her. Stacy was wearing a pink dress with three ruffles on the skirt and pink heels. I wondered if Stacy had heels in every color. But I had to admit that she looked great.

Alec and Stacy danced right by me. I just wanted to disappear. I hoped they wouldn't see me. I mean, not only was I not dancing, but I was standing there all by myself. I didn't even have anyone to talk to. Katie was with Sam, and Al and Randy were fiddling around with all the lighting stuff.

The song ended. I just stood there, trying to figure out what to do. Before I could budge, Alec and Stacy were standing right next to me. I tried to make a quick getaway, but I tripped over Stacy's foot by mistake. *Oh, great*, I thought.

"Wild outfit," Stacy said as she looked me up and down. Her voice dripped with sarcasm.

Actually, I kind of liked what I was wearing. It was different, that was for sure. I had on these leopard leggings of Randy's with a black cropped T-shirt and a black mini-skirt, white sneakers, and some really strange, really large leopard hoop earrings, also courtesy of Randy. I thought I looked very downtown New York.

Alec was looking at me, too. He had this weird expression on his face. I don't think he liked my outfit, either.

"I like Sabrina's stockings," Alec suddenly shocked me by saying. "They're different."

Stacy glared at Alec. "I prefer a more sophisticated look myself," Stacy said.

"I've got to go," I said quickly to Stacy and Alec. I took off toward the stage, elbowing my way through the throng of kids. Everybody was laughing and dancing and talking. I caught a glimpse of Katie and Sam again. They looked like they were having a great time. I had to get out of there. I guess I just wasn't cut out for junior high mixers. The tears started to well up in my eyes. I couldn't take this for much longer.

When I got to the back of the stage, I could see that Randy and Al were engrossed in whatever they were doing with the light board. They had their heads together and they were flipping all these switches around.

"Guys," I said softly.

They didn't look up.

"Guys," I said again.

They still didn't look up. They were concentrating on the lights and I could tell they were having a good time. They really didn't need my help. I felt kind of uncomfortable standing there with nothing to do. I decided that I'd had enough of this homecoming dance stuff. I had to get out of there.

I drifted slowly toward the wall and began to move in the direction of the exit at the back of the gym. I didn't want to give the impression that I was leaving because I didn't want anyone to stop me. I just wanted to go home and forget that this had ever happened.

Suddenly, the lights went down and one spotlight was trained on Spike.

"I'd like to dedicate this next song," Spike began in that dreamy voice of his that gave me goose bumps, "to a very special person."

A ripple ran through the crowd. I wondered who this special person was. Whoever she was, she was really lucky.

I continued to move toward the exit. I hoped I could make it out before I found out who Spike's special girl was. It seemed as if everybody had someone special tonight, except for me.

"This song is for Sabrina," Spike kind of crooned into the microphone.

Me?! I almost died. Spike was dedicating a song to *me?* I was in shock. Nobody had ever dedicated anything to me before. I didn't even know what to do.

"Where is Sabrina?" Spike crooned. He turned to Randy and Allison. "Can we put a spot on her out there?"

Before I knew what was happening, I found myself in the middle of the gym. There was a huge spotlight shining right on me. It was so embarrassing.

Then the band started to play "Crazy for You." I loved that song.

"Do you want to dance, Sabrina?" a voice suddenly said from right behind me.

I turned quickly. I almost fainted. It was

Nick!

"I mean, this is your song and all," Nick continued. He just looked at me and grinned.

I took a step forward. And Nick took a step toward me. I couldn't believe this was happening. He smiled at me and put his arms around my waist.

"Listen," Nick began with this serious expression on his face, "it was a really rotten thing I did to you this afternoon. I'm sorry. I just got mad when I saw you dancing with that Spike character."

"Yeah, Nick," I said, "it was a really mean thing to do and I really shouldn't even speak to you. Besides, who'd you bring to the dance?"

Nick started to blush, "Well, uhmm, Sabrina, see, I didn't really ask anybody else. I just got so mad when I saw you dancing with Spike that I thought I'd try to make you mad, too."

Wow! That's funny, I never thought boys did stuff like that. I mean, I never thought that a boy would try to make a girl jealous just because he was mad at her.

When I looked back up at Nick, he had this really worried look on his face, then he asked, "Friends?"

"Friends," I said and smiled at him.

"What sign are you?" I suddenly asked. I had to know.

"Sign?" Nick repeated.

"Yeah, you know. Zodiac sign," I explained.

"Cancer," Nick said. "Is that good or bad?"

"It's perfect," I replied. So my horoscope had been right all along. I just had the wrong guy! Well, I'll take Nick over Alec, any day. Any guy that likes Stacy the Great can't be right for me.

Suddenly, I caught a glimpse of Alec. He had this funny look on his face, and he was just staring at us.

"Nick," I said. "I have to do something. I'll be back in a minute."

I walked toward the stage where Katie, Randy, and Allison were sitting. When I got up to them, they all had big grins on their faces.

"Who asked Spike to do that?" I asked them.

"Well," Katie began. "It was Randy's idea."

I looked at Randy in shock. "Thanks, Ran. That was great!"

"Hope you liked the smoke," Randy said, trying to change the subject.

"How did you guys find me with that spot?" I asked.

"I was watching you," Allison replied. "I figured you were trying to sneak out."

That Allison, she's amazing!

"Yeah," said Randy, "and we thought you were going to miss your big moment. It was mighty close."

I smiled at them. I was so happy I could cry. Katie, Randy, and Al were the absolute best.

Randy put her arm around me and squeezed my shoulder. "Welcome to junior high, kiddo," she said.

Titles in the GIRL TALK series

⟨1⟩ **WELCOME TO JUNIOR HIGH!**
Introducing the Girl Talk characters, Sabrina Wells, Katie Campbell, Randy Zak, and Allison Cloud. When our four heroines meet and have to plan the decorations for the first junior high dance of the year, the results are hilarious.

⟨2⟩ **FACE-OFF!**
Katie Campbell is just plain fed up with being "perfect." But when she decides to join the boys' ice hockey team, she gets more than she bargained for.

⟨3⟩ **THE NEW YOU**
Allison Cloud is down in the dumps, and her friends decide she needs a makeover, just in time for a real live magazine shoot!

⟨4⟩ **REBEL, REBEL**
Randy Zak is acting even stranger than usual — could her dad's trip to Acorn Falls have something to do with it?

⟨5⟩ **IT'S ALL IN THE STARS**
Sabrina Wells's twin brother, Sam, enlists the aid of the class nerd, Winslow, to play a practical joke on her. The problem is, Winslow takes it seriously!

⟨6⟩ **THE GHOST OF EAGLE MOUNTAIN**
The girls go camping, only to discover that they're sleeping on the very spot where the Ghost of Eagle Mountain wanders!

LOOK FOR THE GIRL TALK BOOKS!
COMING SOON TO A BOOKSTORE NEAR YOU!

LOOK FOR THESE GIRL TALK
GAMES AND PRODUCTS!

Girl Talk Games:
- Girl Talk Game
- Girl Talk Second Edition
- Girl Talk Travel Game
- Girl Talk Date Line

Girl Talk Puzzles:
- Hunk
- Heart to Heart

The Girl Talk Collection:
- Blushers
- Lip Gloss
- Hair Fashions
- 20 Anywhere Stickers
- Slumber Party Kit
- Eye Shadow
- Fingernails
- Paints that Puff
- Fantasy Fortune Party Kit

TALK BACK!

TELL US WHAT YOU THINK ABOUT GIRL TALK

Name _____

Address _____

City _____ State _____ Zip _____

Birthday: Day _____ Mo _____ Year _____

Telephone Number (____) _____

1) On a scale of 1 (The Pits) to 5 (The Max),
how would you rate Girl Talk?   Circle One:

        1   2   3   4   5

2) What do you like most about Girl Talk?

___Characters___Situations___Telephone Talk

Other _____

3) Who is your favorite character?   Circle One:

    Sabrina   Katie   Randy

    Allison   Stacy   Other

4) Who is your least favorite character?

_____

5) What do you want to read about in Girl Talk?

_____

_____

Send completed form to :
Western Publishing Company, Inc.
1220 Mound Avenue Mail Station #85
Racine, Wisconsin 53404